Joan London is the author of two prize-winning collections of stories, *Sister Ships*, which won the *Age* Book of the Year in 1986, and *Letter to Constantine*, which won the Steele Rudd Award in 1994 and the West Australian Premier's Award for Fiction. These stories have been published in one volume as *The New Dark Age*. Her first novel, *Gilgamesh*, won the *Age* Book of the Year for Fiction in 2002 and was long-listed for the Orange Prize and the International IMPAC Dublin Literary Award. Her second novel, *The Good Parents*, won the 2009 Christina Stead Prize for fiction. Joan London's books have all been published internationally to critical acclaim. *The Golden Age* is her third novel.

Praise for *The Golden Age*

'Outstanding . . . fearless, graceful and deeply benevolent'
Helen Garner, *Australian* (Books of the Year)

'London is my favourite Australian writer; her prose is matchless in its precision, beauty and clear-eyed compassion'
Charlotte Wood, *Sydney Morning Herald* (Books of the Year)

'It is a measure of London's deftness as a storyteller that the novel is also a universal meditation on nostalgia and hope, belonging and exile, love and loss, old world and new. Indeed, for a relatively short work it contains multitudes: narratives overlaid and assembled in such a way as to link disparate characters, milieus, generations, their respective fates imbricated like tiles on a roof. This sense of compression is aided by prose that often feels closer to poetry, that most direct of routes by which language gets to the truth of things . . . Third-person perspective allows her to track swiftly, cinematically, between characters. And yet such authorial attentions are so empathetic and minutely rendered in psychological terms, it is as if the novelistic intelligence has merged, momentarily, with its creation' Geordie Williamson, *Australian*

'This novel is a brilliant display of life and change: the transition between war and peace, between love and permission, between terrible paralysis of various kinds and movement' Brenda Walker, *The Monthly*

'[London's] writing, which calls attention to itself only by its precision, gives you an opportunity, the way silence sometimes does, to reflect productively. Best of all, it returns you to an early pleasure: the pleasure of story, of wanting to know what happens next . . . Comparisons have been made before to the work of Alice Munro, and indeed London has that same respect for every character that Munro does . . . a book that carries the quiet assurance of a classic, which it will most certainly become' Tegan Bennett Daylight, *Sydney Review of Books*

'Like Chekhov's, London's canvas is also broad. However, she is neither tough nor unsentimental. Her characters each have their stories. What texture this brings to the page and to the reader' *Newtown Review of Books*

'London writes mesmerising stories in lovely, restrained prose' Agnes Nieuwenhuizen, *Australian* (Books of the Year)

'Few write as poetically and as truthfully as London, whose yearning characters are charged with a vivid humanity' Susan Johnson, *Sunday Territorian*

'There is poetry on every page of this book ... the scents and sounds of Perth on summer days, the joy that the children feel on a beach outing, the way Frank's parents are gradually absorbed into Australian life, and how Frank and Elsa become soulmates. Just like all good poetry, London's words tell a story at multiple levels' *Good Reading*

'Joan London's long-awaited third novel has been worth waiting for. It is a tribute to Joan London's writing skills that the reader really cares what happens to Frank and Elsa, especially after they are brutally torn apart. It is a novel to stir the soul' *Ballarat Courier*

'Joan London is a superlative writer. *The Golden Age*, her latest novel, is set in Perth during the polio epidemic. It's pitch perfect and word perfect. And in writing about children and illness London pays young people the respect of giving them total composure and self-hood' Sophie Cunningham, *Australian* (Books of the Year)

Also by Joan London

The
GOLDEN
AGE
JOAN LONDON

VINTAGE BOOKS
Australia

A Vintage book
Published by Random House Australia Pty Ltd
Level 3, 100 Pacific Highway, North Sydney NSW 2060
www.randomhouse.com.au

Penguin
Random House
RANDOM HOUSE BOOKS

First published by Vintage in 2014
This edition published by Vintage in 2015

Random House Books is part of the Penguin Random House group of
companies whose addresses can be found at global.penguinrandomhouse.com.

Addresses for companies within the Random House Group can be found at
www.randomhouse.com.au/offices

National Library of Australia
Cataloguing-in-Publication entry

London, Joan, 1948-, author
The Golden Age/Joan London
ISBN 978 0 85798 900 0 (paperback)
Poliomyelitis Patients – Fiction.
Hospitals, Convalescent – Western Australia – Perth – Fiction
A823.3

Cover image © *Dieter on the train, Sweden 1984* by Nan Goldin, courtesy of
Nan Goldin Studio
Cover design by Sandy Cull, gogogingko
Typeset in Garamond by Midland Typesetters, Australia
Printed in Australia by Griffin Press, an accredited ISO AS/NZS 14001:2004
Environmental Management System printer

Random House Australia uses papers that are natural, renewable and recyclable
products and made from wood grown in sustainable forests. The logging and
manufacturing processes are expected to conform to the environmental regulations
of the country of origin.

The Golden Age is based on an actual children's polio convalescent home of that name, which existed from 1949 until 1959 in Leederville, Western Australia. However, none of the characters in the novel bears any deliberate resemblance to staff or patients and their families who were connected with the home.

For my three sisters

1.

Light

One afternoon during rest-time, the new boy, Frank Gold, left his bed, lowered himself into his wheelchair and glided down the corridor. There was nobody around. It was early December, already hot, and Frank, veteran by now of hospital life, knew the nurses would be upstairs in front of their fan. The door to Sister Penny's office was closed: she'd be catching forty winks on her couch.

His first goal, as usual, was to set eyes on Elsa. He peered into Girls through the crack between the hinges of the half-open door. Elsa's bed was behind the door. He liked to see her face asleep. Even if her head was turned away into the pillow, the sight of her thick gold-brown plait somehow gave him hope. But this afternoon her bed was empty.

1

He rolled on, past the silent kitchen with its bare, scrubbed benches. Even the flies were sleeping. It was as if the whole place were under a spell. Only he had escaped . . .

He'd been waiting for this moment. In his pocket was a cigarette and a little sheaf of matches, stolen from his mother during her last visit. She'd slipped off to have a word with Sister Penny, leaving her handbag on his bed. Later, he thought of her standing on the station platform in the twilight, delving for her matches, dying for a smoke. Visits upset Ida. She didn't come every week.

But the act of taking them was like reclaiming something. He was turning back into his old, sneaky self. He felt suddenly at ease, in charge again. Sneakiness was a form of privacy, and privacy here was the first loss. A resistance to the babyishness of this place, its pygmy toilets, its naps and rules, half-hospital, half-nursery school, and his feeling of demotion when he was sent here.

'We are so very glad to have you,' Sister Penny had said firmly when the ambulance delivered him. 'The younger children do look up to the older ones as examples.'

Frank searched her radiant face and knew there was nothing there for him to test. Everything had been resolved a long time ago.

He felt like a pirate landing on an island of little maimed animals. A great wave had swept them up and dumped them here. All of them, like him, stranded, wanting to go home.

Now he was gliding down the ramp of the Covered Way, past the New Treatment Block, out to the clothes lines, hidden behind a wire trellis, the only place where he wouldn't be seen. The washing had been taken in, dried stiff by lunchtime. The ceaseless rumbling and throbbing of the Netting Factory across the road was louder out here. It was like entering the territory of a huge caged animal. Even the white glare cheered him. Ever since the fever of polio had subsided, light had seemed less bright to him, older, sadder.

Moments of solitude were rare and must be grasped with both hands. He put the cigarette into his mouth and struck and struck the row of flimsy matches, one after another. Sweat trickled into his eyes, his hands shook, he wanted, unreasonably, to curse Ida.

A man's shadow blocked out the glare. A huge pair of red hands was cupping a lick of flame. 'Light?' Norm White-house growled. Frank inhaled, his head spun, his heart surged with love. He knew now why everyone loved Norm, the gardener, who just as silently ambled off. As if to say: a man has a right to a smoke in peace.

The next moment the cigarette was stubbed out on the post of the washing line and thrown across the fence. Frank thought he might be sick. Dizzy, blinded, he veered back down the dark corridor, heaved himself onto the bed. His body was not a normal boy's any more.

He wasn't a little kid either, smelling of soap, asleep like those around him. Yet after a while, as his heart slowed, a smile spread across his face. He could still hear the rumble of Norm's voice.

'Light?'

He may as well have said: 'Life?'

But where was Elsa?

2.

The Golden Age

Because he was so small and undeveloped for his age, Frank Gold, though nearly thirteen, had been admitted as a patient at the Golden Age. It was agreed, unanimously, at the IDB (Infectious Diseases Branch of the Royal Perth Hospital) that it really wasn't suitable for him to stay amongst adult patients. Also, his parents were New Australians who both worked, and had no other family members to help with his care. He needed the nurturing atmosphere of the Golden Age, and supervision with schoolwork. Arrangements were made almost immediately, and he was delivered there by ambulance that same afternoon.

Elsa Briggs was twelve and a half, but her mother had a little baby and couldn't look after her at home. The other patients were younger, from all over the state: from Wiluna in the desert, from Broome up the coast, from Rawlinna, a siding on the Trans-Australia line. Nowhere, it seemed, was too remote for the polio virus to find you.

'The Golden Age' had been built as a pub at the turn of the century, in Leederville, five minutes' walk from the railway station, two stops out from the city centre. It stood alone, bounded by four flat roads, like an island, which in its present incarnation seemed to symbolise its apartness, a natural quarantine. Three of the roads were lined with modest suburban houses, each one drawn back behind a stretch of dry lawn, a porch and front windows sealed by venetian blinds. Along the fourth road the two-storey WA Wire Netting Factory pounded and throbbed twenty-four hours a day. Some considered that this wasn't a suitable location for a hospital. But the children found the noise soothing and loved the lights shining all night through their windows.

The pub had been bought by the Health Department in 1949 and converted into The Golden Age Children's Polio Convalescent Home, to service the years of the great epidemics. Inside, with its ramps and bars and walkways, its schoolteacher, trained nurses and full-time physiotherapist, it was a modern treatment centre, which could accommodate up to fourteen children, some from the country, some who could not be cared for at home.

Outside, rearing up above the dusty, treeless crossroads, it still looked like a country pub. Brick, two storey, the wide upstairs balcony shaded the verandah beneath. It had thick walls for coolness, long alcoved windows, a sheltering iron roof like a hat pulled down low. Wheelchairs rolled easily along the wide, shadowy passageways, over the old polished jarrah boards. The very plainness and familiarity of its exterior seemed to proclaim its function, to give fair shelter and homely comfort. A watering hole.

The name, inherited, could be considered tactless by some, even cruelly ironic. These children were impaired as no one could ever wish a child to be. But perhaps because of its former role, its solid and generous air, it was a cheerful place. The children were no longer sick, but in need of help to find their way back into the world.

The staff and parents were well pleased with the Golden Age. Its rooms were spacious, cool and high-ceilinged. The children were surrounded by faces shining with hope and encouragement. Even Ida Gold (known as Princess Ida to the staff), though never slow to find fault, had to admit that she was grateful for the haven it provided.

The children enjoyed the benevolence of the attention. Here, they were not a worry or a burden to make their mothers sigh with weariness. They felt different – exclusive, like a family – from the day kids, who lived at home and arrived by ambulance for schoolwork and therapy. All through the morning, children came and went between the schoolroom and the New Treatment Centre.

As for Frank, he was a new boy again, working out how to be himself. He was desperate to be normal. Finding his feet, this time, meant learning how to walk. He resolved to behave well because he didn't want another expulsion.

Also, in bed at night, and sometimes in the day when it was quiet, he could hear the distant whistle and hooting of the trains pulling in and out of the Leederville station, which always reassured him.

Above all, he didn't want to leave Elsa.

A line ran through his head, which might be the start of a poem.

Your bed was empty today
when I looked for you.
Why?

Polio had taken his legs, but given him his vocation: poet.

3.

Elsa

Elsa was with Rayma Colley in the Babies Room. The thin wail had wafted across the corridor in the afternoon stillness and seeped into Elsa's head. Finally she'd left her bed and wheeled her way to Rayma's cot.

'Stop that,' she whispered to Rayma, peering through the bars of the cot. Her tone was firm. Elsa was not sentimental about babies. She couldn't remember a time when she hadn't had a younger sister to look after. The first thing to do was to stop the crying. She put a finger in her own mouth, puffed her cheeks and pulled the finger out with a pop. Rayma paused, mid-wail. Her little dark face was wet, her eyes swollen.

You had to make them think of something else.

'Come on,' Elsa said. She lowered the bars at the side of the cot, reached across and undid Rayma's splints. By leaning onto the mattress for support, she was able to drag the little girl to her and pull her onto her lap. Hiccups juddered the tiny body.

Tucking her chin over Rayma's shoulder to hold her, Elsa rolled over to the window. She lifted one of the long white curtains and pulled it around the wheelchair so that she and Rayma were screened off from the rest of the room. All their world now was the view, shaded by the verandah, the slice of empty road and the houses along it, a scene as remote to them as the other side of the world.

'Look,' she instructed Rayma, pointing upwards. The afternoon whiteness had taken on a steely cast, a thin, ragged cloud flitted across their view. The sea breeze must be in. During the long days in hospital, the sky passing across the high window in the Isolation Ward had become Elsa's backyard, her freedom, her picture show. Watched, the sky slowed itself to a silent, endless semaphore of shapes and colours, as if it were signalling a message. She was amazed at how she had neglected it in all her years free to roam, with the sun on her face, the wind past her ears.

'Your mother looks at the sky and she thinks of you,' she said to Rayma. She spoke firmly, looking into Rayma's big, frightened eyes. For of course it was her mother whom Rayma cried for. It always was. In the Isolation Ward, Elsa had listened all day for her mother's cloppity footsteps down the corridor, hurrying in her old orthopaedic shoes to find her, waving to her through the glass panel, smiling, trying not to look sad.

And because the sky had become so important, the two – mother and sky – grew to be entwined in Elsa's thoughts. When she looked at the sky she thought of her mother, and it seemed to be telling her that some feelings would never change and never die. If her mother didn't come, the sky also told her that each person was alone and the world went on, no matter what was happening to you.

When at last she'd left the Isolation Ward and her parents were allowed to sit by her bed, they looked smaller to her, aged by the terror they had suffered, old, shrunken, ill-at-ease.

Something had happened to her which she didn't yet understand. As if she'd gone away and come back distant from everybody.

Rayma had to learn to be alone. Without your mother, you had to think.

It was like letting go of a hand, jumping off the high board, walking by yourself to school. Once you'd done it, you were never afraid of it again.

All the kids could identify their mothers' footsteps. They all longed for their mothers, except Frank Gold, who said he'd rather his father came.

Sometimes even now in the Golden Age, after her mother visited, Elsa had the funny feeling that there was another mother waiting for her, blurred, gentle, beautiful as an angel, with an angel's perfect understanding.

4.

Cockatoos

Black cockatoos flew over the stout brick chimneys of the Golden Age as the children ate their dinners – macaroni cheese – on trays, in their beds. They heard their cries and looked towards the windows but could not see the large black birds swirling and dispersing over the Netting Factory and across the railway line. Bathed and combed, the children were content to eat in silence. Whether they came from the suburbs or the country, they knew the sound as homely, comforting, a good omen, predicting rain.

The Golds heard them as they passed over the roof of their house in North Perth, two stops by train from the Golden Age and a mile's walk up Fitzgerald Street. Meyer was in his tiny front yard, smoking and watering his vegetable patch. The cockatoos were heading for the park opposite and the nuts in the pine trees. They sounded like a hundred little wheels that needed oiling, Meyer thought.

At the kitchen table, Ida, also smoking, thought the cries were melancholy, harsh, echoing into emptiness, an Australian sound.

She and Meyer had wanted to go to America. They waited for months in Vienna to hear from a cousin of Meyer's father who'd migrated to New York in his youth. Finally, at the end of '46, a sponsorship was offered from Western Australia. In Vienna they were living in a dormitory with only a curtain between them and fifty other people. Some had been there for years. So they accepted. When at last they landed in Fremantle, Ida wanted to get straight back onto the ship.

Every day, Ida found something that proved their voyage had been ill-fated. If she missed a bus, it was because they should never have come here. Once, after a visit to see Frank, they'd sat at the kitchen table drinking brandy. Ida talked of the old days, when she used to catch the train and bribe the commandant of the work camp to give Meyer a food parcel. One day in a street in Buda, dressed like an old peasant woman with a scarf across her face, holding Frank by the hand, she had come across Meyer's brother, Gyuri, a butcher, who was carving up the carcass of a frozen horse surrounded by a silent waiting crowd. He told her he'd had word that Meyer was alive.

But here they were, in a free, democratic country, and they were gutted, feeble, shellshocked. Frank had been a resilient little fellow, he'd survived cellars, ceilings, bombing, near starvation. Then they came here.

'Ida,' Meyer said. 'Polio is in every country in the world.'

'Play the piano,' he said. She didn't answer. The reason they'd rented this little half-house was the piano in the dining room. They'd paid for the piano tuner themselves. But ever since Frank fell sick, Ida hadn't touched it.

'Why, Ida?' Meyer asked. He never dreamt how much he'd miss the driven sound of Ida's scales, daily, over and over, a morning carillon.

She shook her head.

He knew the reason. Once, before they were engaged, flushed and heightened after her final, stunning performance at the Academy, she'd admitted to him shyly that although she was anti-religion, she sometimes believed that her gift, in its insistence, its surprisingness, came from God. Playing was a sort of conversation, she said, embarrassed.

It was what was most mysterious about her, most alluring, and, in her daily struggle to be equal to it, most endearing.

Now she was a bird who refused to sing.

'Go to bed,' he said. 'You are tired.'

But she shook her head. If she was tired, the dreams were worse. She poured herself another glass of brandy.

5.

Frank's Vocation

Frank was very happy with his vocation. He'd always sensed that he had one, but he hadn't known what it was. It wasn't music, though Ida's dream had been to produce a prodigy. He hadn't inherited Meyer's hand–eye co-ordination either.

But there'd always been something that accompanied him, ever since he could remember. A secret longing. He'd felt it as a lack more than anything else.

Now that he knew he was a poet, he felt stronger. His future had been restored to him. He felt adult, solid, the equal of anyone on earth. He could overcome any hardship because he had a vocation.

Though, like his past in Hungary, it was something he didn't talk about.

*

There was one reliable gap in the Golden Age routine, between dinner and lights out, into which Frank could disappear. After the trays were taken, before the splints were put on, for twenty minutes or so the patients were left to themselves. Sometimes the boys read – much-handled Spider-Man comics, Enid Blyton, Biggles, *Treasure Island* – sometimes they fooled about with spitball fights. Recently Malcolm Poole had been taking himself over to Warren Barrett's bed – they had a craze for Monopoly. Lewis took out his stamp collection.

It was late twilight. Sounds of laughter drifted down the stairs from the staff quarters, where the nurses were eating their dinner. Soon, in a bright swarm they would descend on the children and leave them splinted, smoothed, kissed, the curtains drawn against the dark.

At this hour, just after sunset, Frank always felt the need to go outside. It was a habit inherited from his parents. Before dinner, unless it was very cold or wet, Ida and Meyer always went out onto their small front porch to smoke and drink an aperitif. Nobody said much. Meyer, cigarette in one hand, glass in the other, stepped into the little front yard, checking out his plants. The streetlights came on with a blink and lit up the last home-going workers passing down Fitzgerald Street. Birds were calling out goodnight as they flew over the tree-tops in the park.

His parents had stood like this at the railing on the deck of the ship to Australia, backs turned to him, their slender drifts of smoke curling up above the horizon like the thread of their own thoughts. There was something lonely yet resolute about the way they stood there. It was not quite hope.

This evening, unobserved, he left his bed and rolled silently out through the open front door, along the verandah. The last streaks of pink and orange cloud were fading over the roof of the Netting Factory. The air smelt of warm dust, with a whiff of Norm's full-blown roses. Tiny birds hunched like a row of knots along the power lines. The first star had appeared.

His poem came back to him out here.

Your bed was empty today
when I looked for you.
Why?

He took his pencil and the half-used prescription pad out of his dressing-gown pocket. It was important to hold on to your words in the way they were given to you. Sullivan had told him that. A notebook was essential. Frank had found the prescription pad in the car park at IDB. A doctor must have dropped it. It was the perfect size for a pocket, and when he pulled it out he felt a little thrill: each blank slip waiting for its instruction, each just the right size for a poem, or the first lines of a poem. For the words of your thoughts.

It occurred to him that this poem could just as easily be about Sullivan, the poet at IDB who had introduced him to his vocation. In fact, as he wrote he realised it was *for* Sullivan, as perhaps all his poems were.

Coming to terms with death is a necessary element in any great poem, Sullivan once said.

And in this matter, Gold, he'd said, rolling his eyes towards Frank, we have had an early advantage.

6.
The Poet

The IDB, where Frank had first been sent for rehabilitation, was a much larger affair than the Golden Age. It
had started life during a smallpox epidemic in 1893 as a
tent hospital in the bushland on the outskirts of Perth.
A new city cemetery was soon established, ominously close
by. As the hospital grew, its wards spread out through the
bush, in long blocks opening onto verandahs. Frank, once
he'd got the hang of a wheelchair, whizzed up and down
the covered walkways that joined the blocks. He visited
wards and kitchens, chased his favourite nurses, chatted to
patients who sat on the verandahs watching the birds dive
in and out of the dark trees.

In recovery he felt a hunger to know why he was alive.

Most of the polio patients were young, single adults,
high-spirited survivors with a taste for sick black jokes.

Frank, the youngest, carried messages, barracked at wheel-chair basketball, helped set up the tricks they played daily on the nurses. Urchin-thin and pale, for a short while he was their mascot, cupid, little brother. He popped up everywhere, disarming critics in his role of The Kid, with something that came easily to him, like a switch turned on inside him, which in later years he identified as charm.

There were moments in the dappled light – the sense of waiting, the endless strangers – that took him back to being very young in the hostel for refugees in Vienna. Saved, but not yet back into real life. Nobody supervised him, he was way behind in his lessons. He loved the freedom. It was as if he'd been granted a reprieve from growing up.

One day he went deeper into the old part of the hospital and pushed through the heavy doors into a ward where four large portholed tanks were lined up like submarines in dock. The room was filled with the sound of their ghostly, rhythmic breathing. Frank stayed very still for a minute in the doorway. Iron lungs, which did your breathing for you. Coffins you lived in. The worst thing that polio could do to you, next to death.

A sweat broke out on his forehead. A ghost-like memory of confinement, of helplessness, ran through his body. He returned to his bed and lay down.

But the next day, as soon as the breakfast trays had been taken, he found himself wheeling back to the iron lung ward.

There was a special, serious calm to the place. It was, Frank saw, the momentary hiatus after the morning flurry of washing and feeding. A single nurse was attending to an occupant at the far end of the room. From the tank closest to the door a head protruded, disembodied on its pillow like a head on a plate. Frank glimpsed a high white forehead, a large clean ear, a Roman nose and chin. Faint acne scars around a pale jawline. The profile of a man, but on a boy's thin neck. He looked like a prefect in sixth form.

'Are you going to come in?' The head spoke calmly, without turning. 'Over here, so we can talk.'

Frank wheeled in beside him. 'How did you see me?'

The young man rolled his eyes upwards. A rectangular mirror was poised like a tipped-up verandah roof above his head.

'Move an inch back. That's it. How old are you?'

'Nearly thirteen.'

'What are you doing here?'

'Looking around. What are you doing?'

'Writing a poem.'

After a moment, Frank said, 'But you can't . . .'

'I write in my head.'

'What's the poem called?'

'"The Snowfield".'

'Snow? In Australia?'

'It's about the ceiling, actually.'

'A poem about a ceiling?' Frank winced at his squeaky voice, his dumb questions. Suddenly he didn't want this role any more.

'I've got the first couple of lines.'

'What are they?'

The poet waited, took a breath.

Overnight
it must have snowed
this is all
I can see now.

'It doesn't rhyme.'

'What makes you think it has to?'

'At school . . .' Frank's voice trailed.

The poet smiled, breathed. '"The Assyrian came down like . . . the wolf on the fold . . . And his cohorts were gleaming in . . . purple and gold."'

He chanted it fast, between breaths, like a nursery rhyme.

'We had to learn that!'

'Of course you did . . . What's your name?'

'Frank Gold.'

'Look, Gold, Lord Byron wrote . . . that poem a hundred and . . . forty years ago. You don't have to . . . write poetry like that . . . any more. Good name by the way . . . Gold. Very . . . *apposite*.'

His name was Sullivan Backhouse. Frank began to visit him every day. Official visiting hours were strict: two afternoons a week, between midday and 1.30. Frank used all his survival skills – intuition, observation, experience – to choose the right moment in each day to enter the ward. After a while he realised that the nurses knew he was there and tolerated him. Or perhaps Sullivan had spoken to them about him. He liked that idea.

They went straight to the point, which was poetry. Sullivan assumed the role of teacher, Frank that of apprentice, though up till now he'd hardly given poetry a moment's thought. In fact, when Ida and Meyer quoted poems in Hungarian to each other, it annoyed him – Ida's holy tone especially.

24

He felt her reverence for music and literature was theatrical, deliberate, and set them even more apart from everyone else.

Poetry didn't have to be about heroics, Sullivan said. It didn't have to strut about. It could sound like someone speaking. It could be about personal things. Big things were happening now in poetry, new movements in the United States. I cut my teeth on the First World War poets, he said – Rosenberg, Sassoon, Owen. They didn't celebrate the war, they talked about the experience of soldiers like themselves, in simple, everyday language. They wrote wherever they were, in dugouts and ships and trains. In hospital. Especially in hospital.

Once you get used to your condition, he said, your imagination becomes free again.

He had always written poems. What about? Frank wanted to know.

'Friends. Sailing. The river in summer. Last day at school. That sort of thing. Nostalgia. Occasional poems. But now it happens all the time. The poems are about the present. The past seems very far away.'

Frank's first impression was right. Sullivan had been a prefect at school. A boy's college. He was captain of the rowing team. They'd been defeated by a whisker in something called the Head of the River. Then Sullivan came down with polio. He'd been going to sit his Leaving and go to university to read English. (*Read* English? But we all do that, Frank thought.) His real love was sailing. He had three brothers, one older, two younger, and they lived in a house with a large garden that ran down to the Swan River. He'd just turned eighteen.

'My father's going to buy me a little one-hander when I'm out of here. So I can get around. As soon as I can swim again.'

After that Frank had a picture in his mind that he associated with Sullivan, a scene glimpsed from a train a few years ago, on the way with his parents to visit Hungarian friends in Midland. An old two-storey house with a wide verandah, a slope of lawn, the sweep of willow fronds across olive-green water. A little jetty with bobbing dinghies and kids in shorts jumping in and out of them. Like a scene in an old-fashioned painting. Of course it wasn't Sullivan's house, which, it turned out, was on the other side of the city, but still it lingered, like a tune or an aroma, set in motion whenever he saw or thought of Sullivan. The sun on the water, the rocking boats, the leaping, leggy kids.

Sullivan's other visitor was his father, who dropped in and out at odd times. There was no question that anyone would deter him. He was tall and long-legged with greying, combed-back hair, formal, in a suit that Meyer would approve of, or sometimes a blue blazer with gold buttons. Matron herself once brought him in. 'Off you go, you rascal,' she'd said to Frank, smiling toothily. Frank, offended, wheeled away at once. He always left when Sullivan's father came. This was a courtesy that all the patients observed when someone had a visitor. Did Matron think he didn't know any better?

But already Mr Backhouse had turned his back on Matron and was bending down to Sullivan. 'How are you, old man?' he murmured, as he always did. He had eyes for nobody else.

Once, at Sullivan's side, perhaps at Sullivan's instigation, he turned to Frank, who was engaged in manoeuvring his leave-taking. 'So you're the youngest patient on the block,' he said, smiling pleasantly. His accent was quite formal, almost English. 'A New Australian.'

'Yes,' Frank said.

'Frank Gold. You are from . . . ?'

'Hungary.'

'Ah.' Mr Backhouse gave a nod. Frank felt the flash of this man's cool eyes. He had been placed.

'When did you come to Australia?' His mouth smiled. His eyes flickered in the effort of concentration on anyone but Sullivan.

'In forty-seven.'

'Like it here in Perth?'

It seemed essential to tell the truth to Sullivan's father, but Frank could not decide how to sum up the experience.

'Yes.' Frank's charm dissolved like morning dew beneath the blaze of this father's bitter desperation. *Why my son? Why can't my boy be sitting there?*

'Good man!' He was already turning back to Sullivan, who always had a joke ready to tell his father, some ward-life anecdote.

Frank saw Sullivan's huge responsibility. *Why do I refuse it?* he thought, wheeling off. His parents, he knew, regarded his lost legs as one more tragedy they had to bear. *I refuse to be their only light. I want to be my own reason for living.* Though Meyer and sometimes Ida came to IDB once a week, he would have preferred them never to visit. He'd entered another world now with Sullivan, an enchantment.

When he once mentioned Sullivan's name to Ida, she frowned. 'Bach-haus? Is that a German name?'

'I don't know!' He shook his head, impatient. 'He's Australian.'

27

'Perhaps it is Swedish,' Ida mused. 'How do you spell it?'

'What does "*apposite*" mean?' Frank asked her, to change the subject.

'It means . . . exactly different . . . on the other side . . . You know that.'

'Not *o*pposite. *A*pposite.' He shook his head again and looked away.

Word got around that Sullivan's father was aide-de-camp to the Governor. That he paid his visits in a chauffeured car. Frank started to wait on the verandah to watch Mr Backhouse leave the ward. Head down, shoulders high, jacket flying, he took long, deliberate strides down to the end of the driveway as if he were picking his way out. A large black Humber was always waiting there.

Sullivan said his real life had always been when he was alone.

'Because you're a poet?' Frank asked.

'No! Isn't it the case with everyone?' Sullivan said. 'Take Sister Addie.' He called her Addie, though she was Palmer to the staff. 'Her face is so gentle and open – have you noticed? All her thoughts are for others.'

Frank had seen only a flat, freckled face between the wings of a cap, also a flat chest and short strong legs in perpetual motion. Not one of the beautiful nurses, the ones they all watched for, longed for. But a smiler.

'I think of her when she's in her room, alone,' Sullivan went on. 'Sitting on the bed, taking off her shoes, rolling down those thick brown stockings. I think of how her face would look then.'

'We die alone,' he said.

Sullivan was always good-humoured. But sometimes he didn't speak when Frank arrived. He blinked a greeting, but lay looking straight ahead. The first time he did this he mouthed at Frank: 'I am working.'

If Frank sat there long enough, Sullivan would start to deliver a line on each out-going breath. Frank wrote them down in his prescription pad.

It turns out that
we are tough
as cockroaches.

A shudder ran through Frank. He still felt too vulnerable. He heard the crunch of carapace, the crack of fragile bones. Like all creatures, human bodies were easily wiped out.

'Don't worry, Gold,' Sullivan said. 'I'll work on it. The lung is a good editor.'

Once, he was very distant. He didn't open his eyes when Frank greeted him. 'He had a bad night,' Sister Addie told Frank as he came in.

Frank waited until she had gone, then bent down to him. 'How are you?'

Sullivan opened one eye.

'Can't pick my nose. Can't scratch my balls or wipe my arse. But apart from that, everything's pretty rosy, Gold.'

He closed his eye and smiled broadly. It seemed to do him good.

Sullivan was getting better. He spent time out of the lung. Five minutes at first, then ten, then one day for half an hour he sat on the verandah strapped up to the neck in a recliner, next to Frank's wheelchair. The sun shone. They sat content with the world, like two old men. 'At last I'm learning how to live,' Sullivan said.

He spoke of the day polio had attacked him. Everyone had their onset story. His began during the famous Head of the River rowing race. He'd felt shivery but thought it was nerves. His boat was a nose ahead, and suddenly he had no more strength to draw on. It was like tugging on a bell-pull and nobody comes, he said. They came in third. At the end he felt so hot and shaky that he thought a swim might help. He didn't care if this was out of bounds, he plunged right into the river. Then he found he couldn't move his legs. He put his hand up, and everyone thought he was joking. By the time they dragged him onto the pontoon, he was struggling with each breath.

He remembered the day with a peculiar vividness. In his mind it had a sort of beauty. He had been very happy at school, and had a deep attachment to two or three of the boys. He believed they'd be his friends for life.

They laid him back on the pontoon and ferried him to shore and he saw the sun glowing through his eyelids and felt its warmth on his body and heard the splashing of the water as the boys waded him in. He heard their silence. And right then and there a poem flashed into his head that was going to say it all. A long, major poem, called 'On My Last Day on Earth'. Everything he wrote now was part of it.

In contrast, Frank's own onset experience had been so unpoetic that he did not want to speak of it, reflecting as it did what he felt to be the loud, raw, over-intimate tragicomedy of his own family life. It involved a blinding headache, his refusal to get up, Ida shouting at him that she was running late and could lose her new job at the milliner's.

Meyer was long gone, working the early shift. Ida stormed off, then returned from the bus stop to check his forehead one last time. Then the sound of her frenzied panting filled their tiny house as she searched for coins in Meyer's pockets, cursing him for never being around when she needed him. She ran down the street to the phone box to call Dr Cohen, leaving the front door wide open.

Then Meyer's miraculous reappearance, lying in his arms like a baby being carried to the ambulance. Meyer's tanned face was a greyish colour, Ida's white as flour. People were watching, the Zanettis, other neighbours, passers-by, a blur of faces at a distance, like a dream.

This will teach them, he'd thought, strangely detached and matter-of-fact. Teach them what? Not to count on him for all their happiness! *I refuse to be their only light.*

One day this too will be a dream, he thought now, his eyes closed in the sun.

'We're getting better,' he told Sullivan in his recliner.

'Or is this just a reprieve?' Sullivan said. A severe cramp had started up in his back and Frank set off at once to find Addie.

One night Frank woke to sticky heat, thick darkness, thunder, lightning flashes, gusts of heavy rain. Not even the dim glow of a night lamp anywhere. The power must have gone off. As he lay there, he remembered that the iron lungs were worked by bellows connected to a large electric motor outside the windows of the ward.

His chair was parked by the door of the ward. He slid from his bed onto the floor and elbowed his way across the cold lino through the door into the walkway. The driving

31

rain sprayed him as he peered into the darkness. There was no sign of life anywhere. Had everyone forgotten the iron lung patients?

In the next lightning flash he saw a flock of white shapes like ghosts advancing through the driving rain. He made out female figures and recognised nurses, all in soaking shortie pajamas, running from their quarters to the iron lung ward, where, he found out the next morning, for three hours they'd hand-pumped the bellows. The moment he saw the nurses' brigade he knew that the lung patients would be all right and, exhausted, he elbowed his way back to his bed.

There was talk of some patients going home for weekends. Not Sullivan, who no longer left the lung, and not Frank, who didn't want to leave Sullivan.

'Slowly I am turning into something else,' Frank wrote, for Sullivan, in the prescription pad. It was the first line of his new poem, called 'What Is Left'.

We have left tragedy
at home with our mothers and fathers.

'My father wants to print my poems,' Sullivan said. 'Just a small, private thing. Not *these* poems. The ones I used to write. About friends and sailing and so on. Rhyming poems. He wants to call it "Youth". I told him I'd like to call it "On My Last Day on Earth", but he won't hear of it. I'd like the book to end with that poem, though it isn't finished yet.'

He closed his eyes for a while, then he opened them at Frank, and said, 'Here's the last line for you, Gold: "In the end we are all orphans."'

The next morning, over the clatter of breakfast trays in his ward, Frank heard one of the nurses remark to another that an iron lung patient had died during the night.

Frank knocked his tray to the floor in his scramble to reach his chair.

'Hey, youngster!' and 'What's up with you?' the other patients called as he wheeled off down the walkway.

Sullivan's iron lung was not there.

'I was coming to tell you,' Addie said. Her nose and eyes were red. Her cap was askew, her shoulders drooped. 'He had a bit of a sniffle, couldn't eat his tea, and then his temperature went sky high.' She clicked her thumb and forefinger together. 'He went, like that.' She stood before Frank, clasping and unclasping her hands.

A line came into Frank's head.

Oh why do you stand like this before me
wringing your little red hands?

'Where is it?' He gestured towards the place where the lung had stood.

'Being serviced. Fumigated. It's needed, Frank.'

Sullivan's father, white-faced, came walking through the ward with Matron, carrying a bag. He stopped when he saw Frank and bowed his head. 'Our dear boy has lost his life,' he said. An act of respect for a friend of his son. An official salute. He lifted his head and walked on.

33

Lost his life. It was as if Sullivan continued, but without his body.

Most of Frank's relatives had been murdered during the war, but he had never felt their loss. He lay on his bed and pulled the prescription pad from his pocket, opened it at the last lines that Sullivan had asked him to record.

I have to find myself
A place where I can breathe.
That's where poetry lives
In the oldest part of us.

Just notes, Gold, he'd said. A lot more work to do.

Frank rang Meyer at work from the phone box in the entrance hall. 'A boy died,' he said. He couldn't say anything else. He felt dizzy, feverish. He was trying to finish a poem. Sullivan's poem, 'On My Last Day on Earth'. It was up to him. All around him he sensed the swirling rhythms of the hospital routine, the walkways like flowing arteries, the thick, breathing darkness of its rooms. And beyond that, the pulsing sun, the birds diving, the mysterious shadow life of the bush. He felt the living, throbbing world, and his own small beating heart no more than an atom within it.

He left the phone hanging and went to his bed, pulling the curtain around him. The old darkness was waiting for him there. He lay rigid on his back, eyes open, arms at his side, barely breathing, as if he too had died.

7.

The Trains

They left in the early evening while there were still some people on the streets, hurrying to reach shelter before dark. The night before, everyone in the big apartment below theirs had been rounded up and taken to the banks of the river. How many? Thirty? Forty? Some were children he'd shared games with.

It was a long time since he'd been outside and everything looked older, sadder. The trees had no leaves and the broken street lamps had no light. He saw water pooled over cobblestones, shadows turning in an alley, arches opening into dingy courtyards. Where there used to be a man selling fruit from a window in a wall there was nothing but a spill of bricks and stones into the gutter. Darkness everywhere.

The cold stung like a slap across his bare legs. He wailed, his tears blown away by gusts of gritty wind. He'd forgotten how huge outside was.

His mother jerked his arm. 'What now?'

'My legs hurt.' He was lost, bewildered, mortified: he was wearing a skirt.

She was taking him to her old piano teacher, Julia Marai, who lived in Buda, on the other side of the river. At the last minute she'd decided it would be safer for them if he was dressed as a girl. If they were stopped he wouldn't be given the physical check that would betray them both. She'd made the skirt this morning from the end of a blanket, but was unable to find a pair of little girl's stockings. His socks were pulled up as high as they could go and his neck wrapped in her scarf as compensation. His knitted cap was pushed far down over his boy ears. A tram was coming. Should they risk it? But as the door opened, Ida saw two pairs of legs in green uniform on the steps and pulled him back.

He saw a little dog curled up on the pavement, but he didn't have time to pat it. Over and over Ida had told him that he must not stop, he must walk as fast as he could. If he needed pee-pee, she said, he must crouch on the ground like a girl.

His mother's high-heeled shoes rang on the pavement and her arm jerked his this way and that to steer him. She didn't look down at him. She was wearing a droopy hat that she'd fixed up for herself and it hid her eyes. All winter she hadn't worn anything on her head because of Meyer in the labour camp. Because if his father didn't have a hat in the freezing mountains of the Ukraine, she said, she didn't want to wear one.

But now she was going to start a job. Her mouth was a straight line, her lips had disappeared. She had become somebody else.

They crossed a great bridge, as wide as a road, looping and silent, hanging in the damp, grey air. There were no cars and almost no other people. His mother walked faster. There was something dangerous about this. It was lighter over the river, but so cold that his legs couldn't move. Footsteps echoed behind them. Suddenly Ida swept him up against her, his legs around her waist. He laid his head on her shoulder and felt her heart thump against his chest. She held her arms around his tiny freezing thighs. He saw the black water moving under the black sky behind them and for a moment he fell asleep.

Julia Marai lived with her companion Hedwiga in a long room on the top of a narrow, five-storey apartment house that stood in a row of other buildings overlooking the embankment above the railway line. By now it was nighttime. They entered a courtyard through an archway, turned left and climbed up an open staircase, storey by storey. As quietly as they could, they passed the balconies that ran along each floor. All the doors of the apartments were closed, the curtains drawn. He lagged, Ida crouched down and gestured for him to climb onto her back. A sickness lurched in his stomach: *she is being too kind* . . . The moment was approaching.

By the last door, on the top landing, she slid him down to his feet, gave three soft knocks, took his hand. She waited, gave three more.

'Will there be cake?' he whispered.

'Who has cake now, Feri?' she hissed, shaking his hand a little to wake him up.

The door opened. A fat woman, her body vast as a wall, stood back to let them pass. It was warmer than outside. The light was dim, from one lamp. They passed a stove, a sink, then turned into a long room filled with furniture, a piano, a big table and chairs. He recoiled a little, as he always did at the smell of other people in crowded rooms. Ripe, adult smells he was used to now – armpits and chamber pots, stewed bones, old shoes, sour, frightened breath. And something else he remembered from a long time ago. Milk. Hot milk.

An old woman with white hair sat further up the room in an armchair next to the piano. As they approached her, he saw the flick of a black tail disappear behind a curtain. His mother had promised him there would be a cat.

'This is Ferenc.' Ida pulled off his cap and touched him on his back to make him bow. But the rock in his stomach did not allow him to lift his eyes.

'I'm a boy,' he muttered.

'Of course you are,' said a deep, formal voice. 'And you shall have your pantaloons back.'

He looked up. The old woman sat hunched and flowing like a mountainside in the half-dark, her black eyes loose around the lower lids, shining, streaming out of her square white face.

Ida, as if obeying an instruction, crouched down, took his woollen pants out of her handbag, pulled them up over his shoes and legs, removed his skirt and handed it to the fat woman, Hedwiga. Also some notes of money. She kissed Julia's hand and, kneeling in front of Frank, reclaimed her scarf from his bird neck. 'Do everything you're told,' she said, slowly for emphasis. 'You're a big boy now.' Her breath smelt of her dry mouth. He knew she was afraid.

38

She left. He ran to the window and looked between the curtains, but darkness had swallowed her. For a few moments he was still with her as she went on her way.

There were no lights to be seen. Without her scarf he felt ice-cold, exposed, adrift. He whimpered a little, but the women appeared to be deaf. He heard a train hooting, then a long, slow wail. There must be a station nearby.

Hedwiga led him by the shoulders to the table and placed him on a chair made higher with two cushions. Before him was a soup bowl of hot milk, half-filled with crusts of soggy bread. In front of his eyes she sprinkled a pinch of precious sugar on top, stood back and watched. He ate it all without looking up. For once there was enough. It filled him with warmth. He sighed. Something frantic in his body was at last at peace. A gleam appeared in Hedwiga's eyes. This was the way she smiled.

She led him to a large wooden trunk against one wall, opened it and showed him a bed made with a quilt and a pillow. He climbed in and fell asleep at once like a little dog with a full stomach.

During the day the lid was closed so no one would know it was a bed. Also he was not allowed to press his face against the windows. Or draw in the frost on the glass. You never knew who might be looking up from the street. And he must never, ever, go outside. He was their secret, Julia said. Something that you never tell, you never show.

Ida had gone alone to ask Julia some weeks before. She'd left Frank playing with the other children: an older girl promised to keep an eye on him. Every minute counted. While the two old women discussed it, Ida had thumped out the opening bars of the 'Hammierklavier' on Julia's piano to give them privacy, feigning indifference to her teacher's ever-critical ear.

'What have we to lose?' Julia said when Ida put her hands back on her lap and swivelled to face them. Ida saw that they were flushed, a fighting light in their eyes. They were pleased to play their part in resistance. But, she knew, their true heroism lay in acquiescing to this intrusion into their peace together, the decades-long sweetness of their routines.

Who would think that one day she would ask this woman, of whom she was in awe, to take in her child? And that Julia, who had no interest in little children, would accept? In these times, kindness and unselfishness were as unexpected, as exhilarating, as genius. By now Ida was used to, indeed expected, near-universal rejection, refusal, contempt.

All the same, only the fact that Ida was Julia's heir, star student, bearer of the standard, allowed her to ask such a favour.

It was her giftedness that saved him.

Now, cut loose, adrift, Ida retraced her steps down the hill, back across the Szabadság bridge – the bridge called Liberty, fifth of the seven great bridges that crossed the Danube between the two sides of the city. To walk across was like a test. Everything seemed to go silent. Footsteps echoed on the bridge as the few pedestrians, faces sunk in scarves, approached and passed each other. She walked so stony-faced beneath her hat that she was almost grimacing, though, who knew, attractiveness might be the only way she could save herself.

Deep in her sad, tight heart, she searched for that little fighting core of survival, of self-love, which she'd always had, and must not now lose. She needed to draw on all her drive and shrewdness if the two of them were to survive.

Simpler now, alone. Motherhood had never sat easily with Ida.

She was no longer Ida Gold, but Terezia Bala. She could not afford to distract herself with worries about Ferenc. About bombing raids that one day soon would target Buda. In the case of bombardments, Julia said, she and Hedwiga would not go down into the cellar beneath the apartments with all the other occupants. Julia's legs no longer worked and Hedwiga would not leave Julia. In fact, since the Germans had arrived in March, Julia never left the flat at all.

Ida did not tell Julia that she'd already taken this into account. She knew that the two old women and the child would never reach the cellar in time. Let alone the cat, which would have to be called for and carried. They would not go without Tibor. But by her calculations the chance of being blown up was slightly less than that of being caught and shot into the Danube.

Besides, it was in places such as cellars that somebody notices the stray child, the 'guest' who is staying with the old ladies, mentions this new 'nephew' to the caretaker, who may have connections with the Arrow Cross . . .

Yes, it was more acceptable to her if her son was killed by a bomb along with everybody else rather than singled out, hunted down and left to drown in the Danube tied to another who had been shot. Two, or even three, for one. In that way, bullets were saved.

That was the choice she'd made. Its awfulness made her dizzy for a moment. Worse, she was not sure Meyer would approve. 'Keep him close.' His last words. He believed that the boy should stay with her.

41

But seeing Julia always hardened her resolve. Julia, who'd insisted on the impossible, on finding your own resources, on surprising yourself. Talent was not enough, Julia used to say, you must find the grip, the hunger, the small, determined child inside you. You must have a certain ruthlessness to win, as if by right. In the hierarchy of talent, you are born an aristocrat . . .

Ida, a Jewish girl, had won the medal at the Liszt Academy, and a standing ovation after her performance. She'd presented the bouquet to Julia.

In a spirit of celebration her father had taken the family on holiday to Lake Balaton, where she'd met Meyer. By the time the laws came in that prohibited her from attending the academy, from teaching or performing, she was in love, about to marry, and so her heart did not break.

Wait, Julia said, this madness will pass. Practise! Practise!

Ida decorated the apartment that her father had given them. She was pregnant, she did not play the piano. Those keys, which only rewarded you with beauty after years of faith and patience, had nothing to do with the mad, sly hostility that was beginning to insinuate itself into their lives, the insults, the exclusions, the peremptory laws . . . This mounting force for which they had no name.

She dreamt of a child like Meyer, but after Ferenc was born she saw that he was pointy-faced, pale and petulant like her and that his first smile, like hers, would always be directed towards Meyer.

The loneliness of being apart from Meyer never left her, as if the warm flesh, the courage of her bones had been stripped from her. Her stomach ached, it hurt to urinate, the quicks of her nails were broken, her gums had shrunk.

When he came back from the work camp, it would be an old woman he took in his arms.

Behind her, to her right, was the great spa hotel, the Gellért, overlooking the Danube. If she stopped, she might catch a few strains of music. The band played on, these days to a new, uniformed clientele.

In '41, through an old friend from the Liszt Academy, she'd had a job playing the piano one afternoon a week in the famous tea-room of the Gellért. One day a waiter delivered a note to her, written in an unknown hand. 'They are going to take you.' She put it down the front of her dress like a billet-doux, her face demure, and broke into a sunny Strauss waltz. To warm applause, she rose, and gaily holding up five fingers to indicate the length of time of her absence, she bowed and slipped out, coatless and unpaid, through the kitchen entrance, across the Szabadság Bridge, back into Pest.

Her new job was in a suburb in Ujpest, which was all but bombed out. Through Suszi, the Christian girlfriend of Meyer's brother Janos, she'd bought papers. Terezia Bala was a milliner from Szentendre, and, as from today, a housekeeper for an old couple. Suszi had given her a cross to wear around her neck and taught her the Hail Mary.

She knew that Meyer was alive in the Ukraine – or rather, she knew he wasn't dead. But the signal was getting weaker. Her nerves were thinned, stretched, waving like antenna. He couldn't hold out much longer. She'd glimpsed him in dreams, trudging past her into a blizzard. He was somewhere in the north-west. She had to find a way to get a food parcel to him. Since Meyer's Christian business partner had requisitioned all their assets, she'd run out of money. Sold everything that was left, her pots and pans, her sheets, Meyer's wedding suit. She had to be free, at least for two or three weeks, to make a little money, to bribe and barter, and get her parcel to Meyer.

How could a city that you loved with all your heart, as a child loves every corner of the old family house, a city of archways, courtyards, boulevards, cafés and concerts, twink-ling bridges and the Castle looking down over the great silver Danube, so that neither Paris nor London held any charm for her, nor Shanghai when Meyer had suggested it . . . how could it turn into a hunting ground, its shadows terrifying, its courtyards traps, its people's faces turned blank to you like hostile children in a schoolyard? Finding her way through these familiar streets had become a game of chance. Even her footsteps sounded frightened. The sun itself seemed wan and bitter, soiled by all it saw.

Each day, something more was taken from you. Now her child.

Just for a couple of weeks, she told herself.

Superstitious like all performers, she couldn't help believ-ing that Julia's presence was protective, that it was lucky, a good omen, a blessing for Ferenc, as it had been for her. Julia would never *allow* a bomb to fall on them . . . Ida could not afford to think about how irrational this was, how Meyer would roll his eyes and shake his head. Or would he, now? By what frail threads of chance or luck had Meyer stayed alive?

*

Could Frank really remember this journey? The cold, the bridge, the dark city? Or was this a story composed from Ida's reminiscences? Her stories grew up with him, they were intertwined with his, part of him, like the food she prepared.

But Julia's apartment was his own memory, that long, high room lodged like an attic in the front part of his brain. Pale light, a little unearthly, changed according to the slow movement of old bodies passing across the windows, often two bodies joined together.

On his first morning he woke early. He left the trunk and tiptoed through the room, past the table, past the piano. Julia and Hedwiga were lying very still, face up in their box bed in the alcove. It was cold. He wondered if they were dead. The cat, Tibor, was lying between them. Tibor's ears twitched, he lifted his head and cocked an eye at the child.

It was the beginning of himself. Up until then he hadn't really felt sad or frightened, his mother had done that for him. As long as she was there, he didn't have to fear. He was part of her, and like a mother cat she had attended to every part of him. Now each morning, while Hedwiga was busy with Julia, he pissed into the chamber-pot and pulled on his own pants. He buttoned up his woollen vest and slowly, seriously, as his mother had instructed him, ran a wet comb through his hair.

For a while he felt a silence in the air around him, an emptiness at his elbow. If he fell over who would pick him up? He had an impulse to crawl, in order to feel safer, but Julia told him to stand up and walk on his two feet. He did everything that Julia told him to do, as his mother had instructed.

How quiet and spacious it was up there after the dark rush of the streets, the tense, packed rooms and cellars of the apartments. The clouds floated by, a bird drifted, a train hooted as it passed. A country of roofs and spires and chimney pots lay below him, like a forest in the winter light. Julia, wrapped in a rug, slept in her chair or read poetry. With cool patience she taught him to play checkers. Every day she played a single game with him.

Hedwiga was a provider. She collected nettles from the embankment and made soup. Grew potatoes in a secret place there, harvested them under cover of darkness. The skins were peeled and dried on the windowsill, to eat when there was nothing else. In the early morning she went out into the mist to trade and barter. She was able to obtain a little milk for Ferenc – Julia insisted he should have milk – and, once, a half-sack of wheat from her village. He helped her grind the wheat on a flat stone with another stone. In the morning she made this into porridge, with milk for him and a pinch of sugar. She was a genius of improvisation. Her food was a sort of happiness. There was no hunger here.

After breakfast came the tremendous work of getting Julia on and off the commode. Hedwiga was very strong, her shoulders broad, her rough hair cut short across her forehead like a child's. The sight of her white, crooked teeth when she ate or spoke was pleasing to Frank. When her small eyes gleamed at him he felt a surge of encouragement.

What if one day Hedwiga, like so many others, did not return from her errands? There would be nothing for him and Julia to eat. But Hedwiga always came back.

There was also the muscular Tibor, rarely seen by day now, since he had to hunt for his own meals. Once they found a large rat laid out on the rug, as if to help them out. This was a rare moment when they all laughed. He liked to tease

46

Tibor by making him chase the long, thin sandbag that kept the draught from blowing under the door. The old ladies tolerated this for a little while. He knew he had to stop when Julia cleared her throat.

He played games with himself on the floor, in a corner beneath the window, something to do with a block of wood he called his cart and fights he tried to engineer between moths and spiders. He heard the drone of planes and ran to the window. Bombing had started up, down the hill, near the river. There was a tremendous noise, then trees and buildings were thrown like toys into the air. Hedwiga dragged him away and covered Julia and him with a blanket in case the glass shattered. When it was over he returned to the window, to resume his watch for Ida.

He could no longer see her face. To him she was always walking just ahead of him, crossing a bridge.

The days passed, life behind glass. Sometimes a beam broke out of the heavy sky, flickered weakly like a moth across the wall, went out. He turned the pages of Julia's book from her childhood, dark paintings of goblins, forests, castles. He heard the trains going in and out of the Déli station.

Then came Thursday.

Julia explained that a man called Mr Arpad had a piano lesson for one hour every Thursday afternoon – she and Hedwiga depended on the money – during which, Ferenc, their secret, would have to hide. It seemed that old Mr Arpad always needed to use the bathroom during his lesson. The only place where Ferenc could hide was in the roof space above the ceiling. He would have to remain very quiet.

'Why can't I see Mr Arpad?'

'He is no friend of yours,' Julia said.

That afternoon, Hedwiga stood with Ferenc on top of the sturdy dining room table and pushed open a trapdoor in the ceiling with a broom handle.

'Up you go,' she said, lifting him around his knees straight into the square black hole.

'No mice, rats or spiders,' Julia called out. 'Tibor has cleaned it out for you.'

It was pitch black. A rug then a pillow were shoved up after him. He was too shocked to protest.

'Lie down,' Hedwiga called, 'and don't move or the ceiling will creak. *Not a sound* . . . As soon as old Arpad leaves I'll come for you. One hour.'

'Go to sleep,' she advised, and shut the trapdoor.

After a while he saw light high up in small cracks between some of the tiles. At this part of the roof, near the trapdoor, he could sit up with his head bent, but not stand. It was very cold and he tried to pull the rug around himself. Dust went into his nose and mouth. He heard Mr Arpad's knock, the door opening and closing, the growl of a man's voice. He heard the piano, stopping and starting, the same piece of music over and over. He lay back in the darkness.

He'd learnt, like all children in those times, to do as he was told. To stay quiet could be a matter of life or death. But the effort of lying still in that space, alone, never left him.

He knew he was not loved by the women. What if they left him there? The roof seemed to be closing down on him. It was getting hard to breathe. His heart was thumping, he did a little piss, he could hear his own breathing getting louder, but he didn't make a sound.

Perhaps he passed out for a moment. When he came to, he heard a train setting off from the Déli station, squealing and clanking, creaking its way out. It was one of the supply trains that he watched passing by every day at the bottom of the embankment. First a long call, slowly fading, then a last blaring of its horn. It sounded lonely, a lost animal in the dark. Next came the shrill whistle and easy rhythm of an express train, busy, dancing, like a girl.

Ida, he knew, shuddered at the sound of trains, which had carried off Meyer, and her father, and so many people she knew. But for him these sounds were comforting, familiar. They were company. He started to listen out for the next train and the next, their urgent calls and counter-calls like voices echoing over the dark, unhappy city.

In that way one hour passed.

But when Hedwiga opened the trapdoor and lifted him down, something had happened to him. For many days he did not speak with his voice. He spoke in his thoughts.

The next Thursday, when Julia told him Mr Arpad would be coming, he crouched in a corner and did not speak or eat. When Hedwiga came to pick him up and lift him into the ceiling, he threw himself back, his legs stiffened and his heels drummed on the floor.

Hedwiga carried him kicking into the bathroom and gave him an old toffee to suck on. She met Mr Arpad at the door and told him that Julia had the grippe and could not give lessons any more.

*

On 29 December 1944, Budapest was encircled by the Red Army. Thirty-three thousand German troops were trapped within the city. By the time the surviving soldiers surrendered on 13 February, Budapest was in ruins. The seven beautiful bridges over the frozen Danube, that united Buda with Pest, had all been destroyed.

The ice had started to break up when Ida, dressed like an old woman with a scarf across her face and stuffing between her shoulder-blades to give her a humpback – dodging the Russians, for even an old woman wasn't safe around them – crossed the Danube by leaping from one chunk of ice to another, along with others desperate to reach Buda.

The roofless shell of Julia's apartment house was still standing. Ida, who had survived not only the relentless shelling of Pest by the Germans, and the starvation and thirst of all its citizens, but also the ceaseless, daily hunts for Jews by the Arrow Cross, made herself walk, without hope, behind the ruins and saw children playing amongst broken masonry. Suddenly Frank came running towards her. Ida's legs folded beneath her, she sank to the ground.

Frank took his mother down to the back cellar where the survivors were living. Hedwiga had carried Julia down the five flights of stairs from the apartment with Frank trailing behind them. No need for secrets any more. Tibor had rushed past them, a sure sign that it was time to leave. He was occasionally spotted amongst the rubble, fat and sleek from eating rats.

They were eking out a sort of gypsy existence amongst the rubble, waiting for the Russians. There was no food, power or water, but because of Hedwiga's skills – her knowledge of wells in the city, her scrounging for wood, acorns and seeds – they had survived.

Sometimes his parents forgot themselves over drinks with Hungarian friends and spoke of the country they once knew – hunting in the forests and sailing on Lake Balaton, the cafés and the concerts, all that they'd loved, all that was lost in this exile. Then they fell silent. They'd been guests, after all, in that country. As they were guests in this one.

Sometimes he, Ida and Meyer said that they were a lucky family, because the three of them had survived and come to live in a free country. Ida always spat three times over her shoulders. Just to put the gods on notice that never again could the Golds be fooled into trusting their good fortune. During the war, apart from two of Meyer's five siblings, he and Ida had lost everyone in their families.

Frank watched Ida's tiny gobs of spit evaporate on the hot red concrete of their porch.

But he could still sense that time in the ceiling somewhere deep in his body. Attics, trapdoors, cinemas activated it for a split-second. His eyes closed and he went blank, as if he'd passed out for a moment. He once sat in the gods in His Majesty's Theatre and had to leave. He avoided tunnels, subways, cubby houses. Refused to play hide-and-seek. Didn't even like reaching under a bed or table.

He felt it as the weak spot, the broken part, the gap that had let polio in.

When he woke it was afternoon and he smelt cigarettes. Meyer was sitting beside him. There was a place, Meyer was saying. Matron had telephoned. An ambulance would take him. The Golden Age. 'You'll be the oldest there instead of the youngest. And it's time you caught up with your lessons.'

Precocious, yet emotionally immature, Matron had said. There was an air of disapproval about her. Meyer was left with a sense of expulsion.

8.

The First Time Frank Saw Elsa

It was early Sunday evening, after visiting hours. Ida and Meyer had gone home and now it was twilight. All afternoon, between two and four, there were clumps of families gathered around a wheelchair, up and down the verandahs, or out on the lawn in Norm Whitehouse's garden. Nella had set out urn tea and biscuits on the kitchen table. It was the first time Frank had seen his parents since coming here.

On the verandah, Ida had made overtures to the family of a little boy called Fabio from the Babies Ward. No one could fail to be touched by Fabio's huge black eyes, a baby creature in captivity, crouched in his father's arms. Even though Fabio's parents were, no doubt, according to Ida, like the Zanettis next door, 'ignorant Tuscan peasants', there was a recognition between them and the Golds, both couples fresh and smart, the women in heels, earrings, the men in light beige trousers and well-pressed shirts. Europeans.

Fabio's mother held out an open box of jellies in the shapes of fruit and shook it, smiling, at the Golds. They discussed *dolce* and *gelati* and the poor, laughable copies found in Perth. 'I crave the *licorice*,' Ida said, waving her arms and pronouncing it in the Italian way. 'But when I bought it here – aargh!' She screwed up her face in an exaggerated fashion. Fabio's mother nodded *si! si!* and laughed delightedly, showing youthful white teeth.

What had got into Ida? She was slightly hysterical. She'd make a remark then take a breath, her eyes wandering. It was a sign of her desperation. She hated it here because Frank said he did. Hated to see her son in a wheelchair, hated the heat, and the bright white light.

When the Golds were alone again, Frank began. It was a place for babies, he said. There was a kindergarten atmosphere. No privacy, nowhere to go, nothing to do. They'd taken him to the Occupational Therapy room and shown him kiddy puzzles and drums and whistles. All to trick you into exercising your muscles. Thank you, he'd told them, I can entertain myself. There was nothing serious to read except a battered set of Arthur Mee's *Children's Encyclopedia* published in 1923!

Ida commented that the artwork in the office was particularly kitsch. Kookaburras and kangaroo paws and little naked black babies.

Meyer remained impassive. 'Give it time, Feri. You need the therapy. The nurses are nice girls.'

'There *is* nowhere else,' Ida said. Her mouth closed tight on all she could have said. Her hand fluttered in her bag and came out empty. She'd light one up as soon as they left.

A tiredness descended on the Golden Age after the visitors departed. The sun was setting and a low, tarnished light crept along the shadowy walls of the corridors. The children, blank-faced, lay on their beds. They felt displaced. Where did they belong? And to whom? They flicked through the comics they'd been given and rustled in their bags of sweets. The ones who had not been visited knew they had to wait until bounty was offered. They lay blankly, forgotten and unloved.

A little girl cried drearily on and on in the Babies Ward. Frank was still getting used to seeing little kids with tiny withered legs in callipers, or strapped up into a frame for the night. It seemed sadder somehow. He knew they cried because they were alone.

But visitors reminded you of how much you had grown apart from them. It was almost a relief when they went home.

Of all the boys in his ward, the one he liked least was in the bed next to him. Warren Barrett was twelve, but big for his age, a man-like maroon tartan dressing gown wrapped around his square frame. The first thing he'd said to Frank was 'How old are you?' then whistled in disbelief. 'S'pose you didn't get enough food over there.'

In another overture he told Frank that he had a cricket bat in his cupboard signed by Keith Miller. Frank said, 'Who's that?' and Warren whistled again. '*Keith Miller!* Right-hand batsman *and* fast bowler! A genuine all-rounder!' Since then a day had not passed when Warren didn't murmur 'Keith Miller!' and grimly shake his head. Frank had been tested and found out, revealing himself as un-Australian. For some reason this gave Warren pleasure.

At this moment Warren was engaged in sucking on a Choo-Choo Bar, his mouth rimmed with black, black dribble dripping on his mustard-check pajamas. Over and over again, Frank thought, he, Meyer and Ida had been forced to live within breathing distance of strangers, like animals in a burrow. Knowing about their underclothes, the smells and habits of their bodies. The little meannesses, the same old jokes, the sulks and temper flurries . . . He experienced an unexpected pang of nostalgia for his parents and the clean, wise way they did things, the three of them facing the world together. He felt alone and trapped here.

There'd been so many places to escape to at IDB. Up the walkways, into the trees . . . But he couldn't afford to think about IDB any more. There was a darkness waiting in the bush around those verandahs, he saw that now. The trees rustled a warning. Death was out there. It had chosen Sullivan. His heart still lurched whenever he thought of Sullivan.

He'd been unable to make any progress with 'On My Last Day on Earth'. Poetry had deserted him. There was no poetry here.

He set off down the corridor to the kitchen. He thought he'd visit Nella, to check out what there was for tea. It always paid to make friends with the cook, wherever you might find yourself. As he passed Girls, he peered inside the open door. Across the room, a girl he hadn't seen before was sitting in a wheelchair beside a window, asleep, her head listing towards the last rays of the sun. Her face, in profile, was outlined by light. Later, he thought that there must have been other girls in the room, lying on their beds, but he didn't notice them. It seemed to him she was alone.

Her legs were long, she was tall, the tallest patient here. Tall as a small woman, but, as far as he could see, with the body of a boy. She was wearing a dress of blue and white stripes with a wide white collar. Her arms were thin and straight, her chest under the collar was almost flat. On her left calf he glimpsed a calliper below her hem, and her right foot was in a plaster cast. Her light golden-brown hair was pulled straight back into a single plait. Little gold wisps escaped and caught the low beams of sun around her forehead. Her skin was very pale.

She looked like a drawing done with a fine lead pencil. He noted the straightness of her nose, her delicate, grave mouth, the clear curve of her jawline, the length of her neck from the bottom of her earlobe to the hollow of her throat. There was shadow between her eye and cheekbone. An aristocrat. Her hands lay in her lap. She was exhausted.

Elsa, he said to himself in the doorway. He'd heard the name mentioned in the course of his few days here, always in a special, peaceful tone. *El-sa*. Like saying *flow-er* or *wa-ter*. He knew this could be nobody else. To his surprise, tears came to his eyes.

Dusk had fallen, a grey translucence that on this one night of the week was not dispersed by the lights of the Netting Factory. Sunday was nearly over. All at once a title came into his head, 'The Third Country'. Everything had changed. His mind was filled with a vision, a distant coastline, a long, gleaming horizon. He fumbled for his prescription pad, but he'd forgotten to put it in his pocket. He could hear someone coming downstairs from the Nurses Quarters. He wheeled off up the corridor back to Boys.

Now it was evening, the light had turned leaden. The pattering started on the verandah roof as they ate Sunday tea – baked beans, jellied fruit and a mug of Akta-Vite – on their trays. After the rain, the air was softer, fresher.

'The Third Country': he was back as the hero in a sort of serial adventure story, a hunt for treasure and a quest for love. He wrote the title in his prescription pad, resting on his dinner tray. The last light was fading in the windows.

For a moment everything at the Golden Age had mystery, glamour. Shadows deepened, the last long beams of light streaked across its polished floorboards.

The tall thin nurse from New Zealand called Ngaire – pronounced Nyree (she always spelt her name out for new patients – N-g-a-i-r-e) – came in to draw the curtains.

That night, for the first time, he dreamt of Sullivan. He was standing with his back turned in water up to his waist – a lake or river – the sky dark, the water glossy, black and still. His arms were held out on either side of him, his hands playing on the surface of the water. His naked body, which Frank had never seen, had the strong shoulders and muscles of a rower, and the hair at the back of his head was no longer worn from lying down.

9.

The Dark Night

Elsa was awake. She'd been dreaming. In her dream she was sitting on the carrier of her father's bike, sheltered from the wind by his toiling, sweating back. They were riding up North Street hill to the beach. The sea breeze was in and the bike veered from left to right with the pump of each leg. Her father was panting, cursing under his breath. It was a hard ride for him, but she knew he'd never, ever ask her to get off. Just as they reached the crest of the hill, before they went coasting down towards that immense, shining horizon, she woke.

She woke at least once every night. It was peaceful, the only time she felt alone here. She had no pain. Her brain was dry and clear as if a sea wind had just swept through it. She felt aware of everything in the world.

The Girls Ward was the brightest of the rooms at night. The glow of the Netting Factory half a block up the street filled the four big windows, dissolving the long white curtains. Its working sounds – stamps and whistles and a rushing beat like the treadle on a giant sewing machine – echoed into the night silence. People were working there, awake. It brought the world to the girls' doorstep. None of them ever complained.

All of them, like her, children of the war and the Depression, had been brought up not to waste electricity. 'Who left the light on? That costs money!' But the Netting Factory stayed lit up all night like a theatre or dancehall or the Royal Show. How many light bulbs were burning? It was breathtakingly extravagant. If you looked behind the curtain you could see the rays of light shooting up to the stars, piercing the darkness. It seemed to be promising something. What? A future. *No one will ever die here.* Or just that life was not so serious after all. That the future was a brightness.

As soon as she came to the Golden Age she'd begun to feel all right.

A dog barked, the curtains stirred. Everyone lay still, strapped up, asleep. Even at night the work went on to straighten their crooked bodies. Their breath was light, cautious. The horror nights were still not far away. The nights with no end, in the isolation ward, when pain drilled into the deepest part of them. All of the girls asleep in the beds around her – Ann Lee, Susan Bennett, even the little ones, Julia Snow and Lucy Boyer – had told their onset stories, but none of them ever spoke of the Isolation Ward. After it was over, like a terrible dream, you couldn't remember much about it. But you were not the same.

There was just one moment that Elsa sometimes returned to, a lurch, a tug of decision she could still feel deep within her. As if there were another person inside her who had suddenly taken charge, a sort of captain who was going to hold on no matter what. The captain was still there. Elsa was not afraid any more.

Sometimes she felt the aloneness of all the kids at the Golden Age, and she wondered how each one had come through. If you didn't hold on to something – a hand, a thought – you would go down.

'Tell me what to do, God,' she'd prayed in the worst time, but there was no answer. There must be some reason, something He wanted, for this pain. 'Jesus!' she'd called, but there was no one. Once she woke out of the darkness to see a tiny man, a gnome or dwarf, perched on her bed-end in the shadows of the night light, one miniature foot tucked confidingly across the other knee. Raucous as a crow, mocking her, screeching 'Give up! Give up!' Who was he? She cried out for water.

As she drank she heard the Irish girl in the next bed being given the Last Rites.

Her mother, Margaret, had stood shivering behind the observation window, tears pouring down her face. Perhaps I am dying, Elsa thought. If she was, she knew her mother would also die.

But the captain told her that was not her concern. Feeling held you back, the voice said. She had to concentrate on this one thing, holding on. She had to cut off from everything else.

She woke one day to the faint shouts of kids in the playing-fields of the school opposite the hospital. It must have been the weekend, there was no noise of traffic. Voices shouting in the wind reminded her of childhood, the lost world of grass and trees, sand and stones. She felt soft and peaceful. The pain had gone.

In the isolation room all was silence. Everything looked different, deeper, shadowed, as if an angel had just passed. Her eyes turned towards the sky in the window, then she realised that she couldn't move her head.

When they raised her to wash her she saw the Irish girl's bed was empty.

Of course! she thought, *he was the Devil, that tiny man who'd come to curse her.* He couldn't take away her life, but he'd taken the body she moved in. If she wanted to, she knew she could turn on the mocking sound again in her head. Once you'd heard it, it was never far away.

And the other? The captain? The voice inside her?

Was that the Holy Ghost?

She heard the clopping hoofs of the milkman's horse, then the clink of bottles as the crates were dropped at the front door of the Golden Age. *Why did I live?* Elsa thought. Prayers had been offered for her at church, her parents said. Prayers had been offered for the Irish girl, too. She no longer asked herself why she'd caught polio. It was too late now, it was part of her.

Polio had taken her legs, made her pale with thin cheeks, and yet, somehow, herself.

'"You are the lucky ones!"' The new boy, Frank Gold, liked to imitate Sister Olive Penny, in a high, strained falsetto. He was the only one here who didn't adore her. 'I bet she gives the same speech whenever a new kid comes,' he said. '"This is a halfway house. Between hospital and home. We don't believe in feeling sorry for ourselves!"'

'She doesn't sound like that!' Elsa said. When she first arrived here from hospital in the ambulance, Sister Penny had put her arms around her and carried her inside. It felt like being loved. In the isolation ward all the nurses had worn masks and gloves.

Also Sister Penny had thick, rosy skin like a peach and naturally curly, honey-coloured hair with a glint of tinsel. The front of her uniform was full and round like the crest of a dove. A little gold watch was pinned there. Prettiness was like a light, it cheered you up.

Frank Gold talked a lot, unlike most boys. But perhaps because she and he were the two oldest patients, he spoke only to her. He was snobby, critical of the other kids. 'A bully boy', he would say, or 'a goody-goody', or 'a sniveller'. Sometimes she thought that if her parents heard him they would say he lacked Christian charity. She told him that herself.

'But I am not a Christian,' he said.

He was not a heathen, but a Jew. She'd never thought of Jews as not being Christian. Jesus was a Jew!

'And you know what happened to him,' Frank said. 'We Jews have to be on the look-out.'

In the isolation ward, he'd believed he was dying of thirst. He thought that he was lying face-up in a blazing sun on the deck of the old Greek ship that had brought him and his parents to Australia. '*Nero, nero,*' he called out, the Greek for water, and the nurses didn't know what he meant.

He's a funny boy, she thought. He didn't look like anyone else. Wherever she went, she saw the long, pale oval of his face, his deep, watchful eyes, the mass of his curly reddish hair. He was always around. From the start he acted as if he knew her. 'Elsa!' he'd hail from down the corridor. As if there were some sort of emergency. He was clever in a way

63

she'd never known before. He could whistle whole phrases of classical music. 'Bach partita,' he'd say offhandedly, or 'Overture to *The Magic Flute*.' Sometimes she saw a look in his eyes that she recognised, the look of someone who has lain in bed thinking, alone, for too many nights.

She heard the sound of footsteps in the hall, the growl of men's voices: the two night-duty policemen from the Oxford Street station calling in on their rounds to see that all was well. They often had a cup of tea in the kitchen with the nurse on night duty. Tonight it was Sister Penny, because all the other nurses, who were young and mostly from the country, had gone to the RSL dance. They'd rustled downstairs and into the wards to say goodnight to the children, showing off their stiff tulle underskirts, their white winklepicker heels, white stoles and corsages of maidenhair fern and rosebuds. They bent to kiss the children, fragrant, excited. Elsa knew that they felt beautiful.

Being here was like a play. The scenes rotated one after another – ward, schoolroom, therapy – across the routines of the day. People came in, said their piece and left the stage. The policemen's voices were fading now. The front door closed behind them. Elsa slept.

10.
The Loving Body

Sister Olive Penny was lying on the couch in her office, the door ajar. She'd done the rounds, taken off her cap, pulled the knitted rug out of the coat cupboard and put it across her legs. It was well after midnight, all the girls had come back from the dance. Upstairs and down, everyone was sleeping. She should close her eyes now for a rest. She kept her shoes on. After twenty years of nursing, one cry and she'd be up.

At this hour the moon shone at a slant through the window, across her well-ordered desk, straight onto her face on the couch. Her eyes opened. She lay trapped in the cold, unearthly light.

In moonlight, you become another self. Alone in a mystery. For a moment the bluish shadows, the sparse room, even the solid old pub window, made her feel she was in a room in a cheap hotel. Well, she'd known a few of those.

It was immediate. It always was. The taller, more thick-set of the two. The new constable, Constable Ryan. Irish name. 'Silver-tongued divils' an Irish nurse once said. The yearning had started. Thought waves. She couldn't help thinking of tom-toms beating out a message.

There was a tap on the window. She woke at once, unsurprised, and stood up. His head was outlined by the Netting Factory light, his face in the dark. She gestured to the left, towards the front door. He was there when she opened it. He came in, shut the door meekly behind him, followed her into the office. The office door locked with the tiniest of clicks. They didn't say a word. There must be speed and no sound. That was understood. Even the ones who weren't bold, and this one was. He was practised, like her. Her head pounded with excuses that might be needed – she heard a noise, called the station – even as he put his arms around her and lowered her back onto the couch. He'd been drinking. Dutch courage. He was used to his strength – in his early thirties, a few years younger than her. Got his experience in the war. His cap lay on her desk. Blue eyes with thick black lashes and fine freckled skin. 'Colin,' she said, remembering his name, rubbing his short black hair.

She knew her cycle, this was a safe time for her. Otherwise she was brisk with contraception, and deft. He had a wife and four small children. There was no risk of VD. She had no illusions about the body's openness to risk. The body had its own rules, like nature, and you broke them at your peril. Her dedication now was to help it to fulfil all its functions. Its needs and loves.

Oh God, it was beautiful.

They were done.

Now was the time she had to rally, pull herself together. He must get out of here. There must be no clinging, no fuzzy promises of meeting again. They would have to see how they felt. Sometimes once was enough, and they were through with each other. She'd had to get used to, and now she loved, this freedom of choice. Like a man's.

She put her soft breasts back in their cups, buttoned her uniform, quickly stuffed a hanky into her knickers and, ridiculous really, pinned her cap back on.

He blew her a kiss from the front step. A seasoned practitioner.

Some weren't very nice people. And some were very nice indeed.

The funny thing was, they never got her wrong. Didn't judge her, didn't think they had to escape her clutches, or even that they should see her again. There was no question of contempt, or talking about her (many were married). Like them, the last thing she wanted was scandal. Number one with her would always be her job and Elizabeth Ann, her daughter.

They knew she met them on the same terms as theirs. According to choice. Instinct. And the hope of something else, different from pleasure. She didn't know what it was. Joy?

She made herself a cup of tea in the kitchen. Ah, tea! The panacea for everything . . . even this faintest sense of loss. She poured a little from the pot into a child's cup, warmed some milk for it and stirred in a spoonful of honey. Just in case. Tenderly she stalked from ward to ward. Yes, Lewis was lying awake, and she propped him up and held the cup to his mouth. Then she stayed with him, sitting by his bed, the back of her hand against his cheek.

It fed into her work, she thought.

She hadn't always been like this. She was a virgin (almost) when she married Alan Penny. It's what you find out about yourself if you're left in the world with a child and no husband. You have no protection. For a while you spin crazily, like a weather-vane open to every wind. You have to be father and mother, woman and man in the world. You begin to find other parts of yourself, less conventional, resources that you didn't know you had.

Alan joined up in '39 and was killed almost at once by a sniper's bullet in Egypt. Elizabeth Ann was four years old. They went to live with Alan's mother, little Enid, in Mount Lawley, sleeping in Alan's room. Olive returned to nursing, at the Repatriation Hospital. After the war they converted the back verandah of Enid's house into a bedsitter. Elizabeth Ann and she would have much preferred their own place, but houses were in short supply. Like men. There were simply not enough to go around.

It began through kindness. Some of her patients, invalided soldiers with permanent injuries, found fitting back into civilian life wasn't easy for them. They'd lost faith in everything, God, wives, government, sometimes even their mates. She was amazed at the loneliness in some men's hearts. Vast as an ocean or a desert: no woman she knew would ever be so lonely.

In the latter years of the war there'd been Mervyn, an American sailor. He had beautiful manners, enthusiasm, and a pleasing hygiene about him, a fresh, clean smell. Though they spoke the same language, he was as exotic to her as a Frenchman. She was forced to hide from Enid some of the

68

presents he gave her for Elizabeth Ann – the little set of binoculars, for instance, with circulating views of Donald Duck and the Grand Canyon, which could only be from an American serviceman. She was beginning to talk to Elizabeth Ann about America, what an exciting place it would be to visit, then the letters stopped coming. There'd been a terrible battle in the Pacific. She would never know if he survived it.

The closest she'd come to a husband was with Harald, and their Wednesday afternoons. It wasn't love – Harald was in his late sixties and had a heart condition and a wife who only knew one thing, how to spend his money – but it was loving. Harald was very appreciative. He shook his sparse white head with admiration for her, her hard work, the good shape she was in, and what he called her pluck. He loved her nurse's hands. Harald was generous too, he helped her sometimes with bills. He made the down-payment on the little second-hand Morris that a friend of his was selling. That car changed her life. But then his heart gave out. She couldn't even go to his funeral.

Enid, though small, was powerful. She let it be known that she had her own views, of which she would rather not speak. Her mouth pursed into little self-satisfied corners, a habit that annoyed Olive.

But Enid had her revenge. She died quickly in late '52, cancer of the womb, and right at the end, when Olive was sitting with her, Enid, with closed eyes, told her that she had left the house to her younger brother, Les, in perpetuity until his death, when it would go to Elizabeth Ann. She thought it was for the best.

'Elizabeth Ann and I won't have a roof over our heads,' Olive told Enid, who pretended not to hear. Her eyes were closed but there was just the faintest twitch to her mouth. The hearing was the last to go.

Elizabeth Ann won a bursary to go to Kindergarten Teachers College. She went to board with the family of her best friend, also a trainee kindergarten teacher. Olive said, 'Your father would be terribly proud of you.'

The truth was, she didn't have the slightest notion of what Alan would have felt about his grown-up daughter. She had her little diamond engagement ring made into stud earrings and gave them to Elizabeth Ann. They suited her. Elizabeth Ann was elfin, like Enid, with serious brown eyes and straight brown hair cut in a deep fringe. She was a quiet, methodical girl, undemonstrative, but a dimple appeared in her left cheek when she was pleased. As they parted, each to her own accommodation, Olive had a funny feeling of *that's that*.

Whenever she had Saturday off, she and Elizabeth Ann met for lunch, at the Kings Park kiosk, or the Palace Hotel, or the Tearooms on the Esplanade. Afterwards they caught a matinee, unless Elizabeth Ann had to finish an assignment. They spoke on the phone on Wednesday evenings. On Sundays Elizabeth Ann went to church with her friend's family, and on Tuesday nights she sang in the church choir.

All Olive had now was a single room upstairs, slightly larger than the surrounding rooms, which were occupied by young women in their twenties. She had a fireplace, never used, and a high narrow bed. They all shared the one bathroom. She rinsed out her smalls every night in the handbasin and hung them out to dry on a little rack she'd bought and set up under her window. To retain some privacy. Kept her bottle of Magic Silver White at the back of the wardrobe. But the offer of this job, after Enid died, had been a godsend. Board and accommodation provided. She could save up at last to buy a house.

The funny thing was, she'd gone into nursing for something to do before she got married and had a family. It was that or office work. Yet it was nursing that sustained her. She didn't even feel like Elizabeth Ann's mother any more, more like a sort of older sister or friendly aunt. She had a sense now that she was going to be one of those who nurse till the end.

These days she thought of herself as a sort of nomad: all she had she carried with her. Strong legs and stomach, steady hands, quick wits, sharp eyes. And her professionalism.

More and more she noticed how much she let her hands do her work for her, how she knew without thinking what was needed. A massage, a warm drink, some cotton wool where the splints were chafing . . . A little chat. It had got to the point when she could often tell if there was something wrong as soon as she entered a room. A voice said, *Do this. Check that.*

Sometimes it seemed to her that this instinct was drawn out of the deepest part of her, like a draught rising up a chimney. She didn't know how this had happened: she was just a silly girl who'd done her Junior and had to earn a living. But this new dimension to her work had become the true source of wonder and satisfaction in her life.

Passing the kitchen door, she saw the two policemen's mugs sitting on the table. She took them to the sink and rinsed them.

11.

Bellbirds

After Sunday, with its anticipations and disappointments, Mondays were a relief. The children, orphans again, woke to the familiar order of their world. As they rolled along the passage to the bathrooms, they passed the open door of the schoolroom, where Mrs Simmons was already writing on the mobile blackboard. As she saw them pass, her rich, musical voice greeted each one of them by name. At nine-thirty the ambulance delivered the day patients, those who lived at home, but were still not able-bodied enough for school in the outside world. All the students who could sit at desks went to the schoolroom, next to the kitchen. The others went to the Girls Ward, where special bed-desks were set up across their legs.

Mrs Simmons liked to begin the day with singing. She started up a song in the classroom and left her assistant,

Rhona Phillips, to conduct while she crossed the corridor and, waiting till they were in time, restarted it in the ward.

'The ash grove how-ow graceful,' the two wards sang, one after the other, in harmony, 'how plain-lee-ee 'tis speaking,' Mrs Simmons's full-throated enthusiasm carrying their shy voices along.

Frank had no idea why Mrs Simmons, clearly of strong character and intellect, would choose a song as silly as this one, but he wouldn't have been Ida's son, waking each morning to fierce scales on the piano, if he hadn't recognised the teacher's perfect pitch, and her ability to keep their thin waverings in tune. 'I love a sunburnt country,' the children sang next, small and pale and crippled, chirping with their bird mouths. Afterwards they felt cheerful and revived, as if they had been running in fresh air.

Workbooks were handed out. The lessons were tailored to each child's needs; the aim was for all of them to rejoin their own age group when they returned to school in the outside world.

Frank's workbook today was Social Studies. Mrs Simmons had ascertained that he was quick with maths but must catch up, as a New Australian, on history and English literature. This morning his task was to memorise the dates of the Monarchs of England and read a poem, Henry Kendall's 'Bellbirds'. He had to write a page on what the poem was about.

Elsa wheeled in and parked at the desk by the door.

'El-sa!' Mrs Simmons called out, her voice soft with liking. 'Good morning to you!'

Elsa nodded, looked down. She really is shy, Frank thought. El-sa, he muttered. Again he heard the special way her name was said.

How could he bother now with the kings and queens of England? He would be tested on them, Mrs Simmons said. He caught her eye and she came over to him. 'What is it, Frank Good-as-Gold?' Already she had a nickname for him, and for all the other students, though not, as far as he could tell, for Elsa.

He loved this. He loved the personal. She bent her head with its coronet of grey-brown plaits and put her large, healthy face close to his. He breathed her warm, spicy smell, studied her hands, the broad backs specked with brown freckles. Mrs Cinnamon, he privately called her. A war widow, with grown-up children. Did she, like his mother's friend Borka, also a widow, have a lover on Tuesday nights and Saturday afternoons? (He'd heard his parents joke about Borka's 'appointments'.) Beneath her full floral skirts her legs were bare, thick and sunburnt, with snaking veins. In each peeptoe of her big white sandals he glimpsed a horny yellow nail.

'These kings of England. I don't see the point.'

'That's our history, Frank. That's where we come from.'

'I don't.' Before he'd come here, he'd never even heard of The Royal Family. Here, they were everywhere. Mugs, pencil cases, newspaper headlines. The King Dies. The Coronation. The Royal Visit. They were like film stars.

'But you're in the British Empire now! She's our Queen too. The British rule the world.'

He couldn't stand the thought that he had come to a country which once again was inferior to another, like a servant or a child. It enraged him. This was a rage that Australians seemed to want to beat out of him. Australians were like good children. They frowned at you if you didn't stand up for 'God Save the Queen' at the start of a picture show.

'No,' he said, 'the Americans do.'

Mrs Simmons raised her eyebrows. 'Not over here they don't.'

One of the day patients called 'Miss! Miss!' and she went.

The day patients irritated Frank, even repelled him. He kept his distance from them. One by one they wheeled in, in leg splints, hand splints, callipers or back braces, a shy, lopsided little company. A reminder to the Golden Age kids of how *they* must look in the outside world. Tragic children, cursed, deformed.

Yet when he thought of Elsa, that he shared her fate, he did not feel that shame.

He looked sideways at her across the wheelchairs, at the calm of her profile. She was reading something in her workbook, one long, slim arm on her desk, the other on her lap. What was she thinking? Why did she seem like a sort of saviour? Like a club he wanted to join. With her you would feel safe, superior.

Therapy always took priority over schooling in the Golden Age. Throughout the morning, students went in and out of class to the Treatment Block. Elsa was summoned. As soon as she left, it seemed to Frank that the room became intolerable. A day kid had to be helped to the toilet. Warren Barrett was made to recite the nine times table. Frank put his fingers in his ears to read 'Bellbirds'. He wanted to hear it. It was cyclostyled in faint purple onto a yellowing sheet. Dozens of kids must have handled it. It was a shame to see a poem so stale and battered.

By channels of coolness the echoes are calling,
And down the dim gorges I hear the creek falling.

How lovely the words were. Poetry gave relief. From what? From everything else.

Yet soon he was caught up in a relentless rhythm, a galloping singsong. Those rhymes! That false arrangement of the words . . .

It lives in the mountain where moss and the sedges
Touch with their beauty the banks and the ledges.

A poem should follow the speaking voice, Sullivan had said.

Mrs Simmons bent down to him. 'How are you going with "Bellbirds", Frank?' She beamed.

'It's very old-fashioned.'

A faint cloud crossed the clear sky of Mrs Simmons's gaze. 'It's a famous Australian poem, Frank. Generations have loved it.'

'Poems don't have to rhyme any more,' Frank began, but he could see she had already lost interest. He wondered whether to tell her he was a poet. A young poet, recently recruited to the ranks of poets, entrusted with a new, secret knowledge.

'Just five lines in your workbook, Frank. Main themes of the poem.' She moved on.

Mrs Simmons didn't understand poetry. Nobody in this room did. Sullivan had opened a door to a world that made everything have meaning, and when he died, it closed behind him.

Frank put his pen down. He had an overwhelming urge to see Elsa, as if only that would save his life. But he was trapped. In this room, in this body, in the will of Mrs Simmons. He picked up his pen and wrote five lines:

'Bellbirds' is a famous Australian poem.
It is about walking in the bush.
The poet is sad that he is old.
The bellbirds awaken his nostalgia.
It was written in the last century.

'You see,' Mrs Simmons said, 'you can do it easily, if you apply yourself.' She read and initialled the workbook without comment. 'How do you know the word "nostalgia", Frank?'

He looked at her. How could he not? Nostalgia was everywhere. It had a special voice, and special time – sunset, Sunday nights. It dimmed the light. Ida's *nostalgie*. *Nostalgie*, *nostalgie*. 'Gloomy Sundays', the Hungarian song that Ida played.

A shadow had come between him and Mrs Simmons. Frank, used to disappointment now in his eternal quest for soulmates, asked to be excused.

But he rolled straight past the lavatories into the Treatment Room.

12.

Angel Wings

Lidja poked her head out from between the pink curtains around the massage table.

'Frank? I didn't send for you.'

'You said I should practise whenever I could.'

'Not during school hours.'

'I've finished my work.'

'Have you got permission?'

'I asked Mrs Simmons.'

'There's no one here to help you, Frank.'

'I want to do it by myself.'

None of the staff could ever resist this.

It wasn't as if anyone else was using the bars. Frank Gold was shrewd as they come, but Lidja decided to let it go.

All the kids felt close to Lidja. She knew them so well, through their bodies, knew exactly how much each could take. Each was an engine in her care and she was a special-ist mechanic. They loved her young broad face, her tanned arms, the white teeth of her smile, her happiness. She sailed each Sunday on the Swan River with her new husband, who was, like her, from the Baltic states. He built boats. She'd met him in the Migrant Camp at Northam. Frank was proud that Lidja too was a New Australian.

Everyone knew that Lidja would never give up on you. She bent their fingers and wrists, twisted their torsos, stretched their legs, brought their heads down to their ribs. They learnt not to whimper or complain. She presided over their momentous occasions – the first time they stood alone, the first step they took.

The reward was Lidja's smile and the way she said their name. She made them feel like athletes training for a race. They must fight, they must never give up, they were going to win!

Lidja disappeared back behind the curtain. From her silence, her still eyes, he could tell she didn't believe him. There was a danger now, he knew, that someone would say: 'That kid is too old and shrewd for this place.'

Frank knew he was shrewd. A long time ago he'd had to learn how to look after himself. But he also considered himself to be an honest person, more than many others, honest to himself.

He needed to find Elsa. Already he couldn't bear to be apart from her for too long, he didn't know why.

Vot da hell, as Meyer often said. It always gave Frank courage.

He looked around. In the New Treatment Room modern sliding windows poured sun onto the massage tables, the full-length mirrors, the rows of parallel bars. This was where the real learning took place. Three hours a day, five days a week. Massage, exercises and salt baths. To become a normal child again. To walk.

The schoolroom was just a way to keep them from forgetting what writing was and classroom manners and mental arithmetic.

Behind the curtain, Lidja was massaging a little kid whose voice was husky from wailing.

'Mama! Mama!'

'Fabio, look! I can lift your leg up now!'

Frank grabbed hold of some bars on the wall and hauled himself up out of the chair. Swaying, knees wobbling, he tried to stand. His body had to remember what that felt like. You had to *think* muscles into action, feel the traces of life within them. He let go and sat down with a thump.

From the therapy bath came the faint, luxurious slap of waves. Elsa.

The Golden Age was proud of the bath. It was custom-made of stainless steel, large, heavy, cruciform, shaped for an adult body lying with outstretched arms.

There was no time to waste. He wheeled across the room.

Elsa was lying in the warm water in her swimsuit, which, like nearly all her clothes, was a hand-me-down from her cousin Jocelyn, Auntie Nance's daughter. The swimsuit of green wool grew dark and heavy in the warm salt water.

On Sunday her father had brought Nance with him on a visit. 'To see for myself,' Nance said.

As they left, Elsa heard Nance say, 'Isn't there an operation she could have, Jack?'

Her voice, its shocked tones, drifted back down the corridor. Her father mumbled something.

'But will she ever walk *normally*?'

Elsa heard the word 'hope'.

Her body floated before her eyes, like a piece of seaweed that could be thrown away. She felt shame for her second-hand swimsuit, for the weight of her useless legs. For the way her father had mumbled to Nance. It was humiliating for him to have a daughter who'd caught polio. She had brought shame on her family. People kept away from families of polio victims.

She hadn't smiled yet today. She floated, pale and grim, with her eyes closed. When she opened them again, she looked straight into the eyes of Frank Gold, peering through the curtains.

The first thing Frank saw when he opened the curtains at the side of the bath was Elsa's foot, floating, her ankle like a wishbone, and the slender knuckles of her toes.

Then the outline of her long pale legs beneath the water, the green blur of her torso, her small head in the support, and her arms spread out on either side, into the crossbar of the bath.

'Angel wings,' Frank said.

'What?'

'The shape of this bath.'

'Oh.'

She closed her eyes again.

He took this chance to study the planes of her face, and her small, determined mouth. His eyes ran down her body again, the pinpoints of her breasts, the V-shape of her crotch, and quickly back to her face.

She opened her eyes. 'I was trying to think of what it was like. Angel wings is perfect.'

Frank was summoning the courage to say that it was she, Elsa, who made him think of an angel, when the curtain jangled on its rings.

'Frank Gold! What are you doing here?'

Lidja, without a smile.

'Talking.'

'A bath is a private business. You know that.' Lidja, always so friendly to the children, seemed seriously displeased. Her tanned face was flushed. 'Off you go, Frank. Skidaddle. Back to school.'

'I've finished . . .' Frank began, but thought better of it. He backed out quickly, without looking at Elsa, and became momentarily tangled in the curtain.

More painful was the way Lidja didn't look at him as he left, but kept her back turned as she dressed Fabio.

An insight came into his head. *He wouldn't last long here.*

Why did his spirits sink? Wasn't that what he wanted? He suddenly felt very tired. He went into the Boys Ward and lay on his bed.

All he knew was that he had no time to lose. For what?

For Elsa.

13.

Meyer Walks Home

Meyer stepped out of the factory into an evening so warm and light that as if by instinct he turned at once towards the river and started to walk. His bus lumbered past as he crossed the Causeway and he felt a lift in his heart, a boy's cap thrown into the air. For what? For himself. He saw watermelon clouds piled up above the dark breast of the river and he smelt the weedy flow of its depths. A fresh-water breeze found him and, like a puppy, licked his face and neck, breathed cool life back into him. Water and summer evenings: ghosts of his past. The natural world, which was all he allowed himself to miss. Balaton. The lake, childhood. His brothers. He always felt better near water.

Generally he left nostalgia to Ida. The past did not deserve it.

Now he'd turned into Riverside Drive and was walking next to the lake-like expanse of water. Far away, along the opposite bank, were the low roofs and trees of South Perth. How flat and spread-out everything was! Little waves slapped against the river wall. Some boys were throwing stones into the water, competing with each other, like boys everywhere in the world. There was nobody else around. A couple of black birds with writhing, hose-like necks bobbed and ducked on the swaying surface. Shags. The ugliness of the name shocked him. He still didn't know the names of most of the birds here. The breeze blew across his face and with every step he felt less tired. He decided to walk home.

Across the Drive was a vast, grassed, nearly deserted foreshore where sporting events or parades were sometimes held. Small planes could even land there. In the middle of the field, a flock of stout crows strutted like black dogs, raucous, demanding, entitled. Nature had never really been contained here. It was a city in which you could still smell grass and dust and the river, like a country town.

At the ferry jetty he turned right into Barrack Street, walked up past the Supreme Court Gardens, across St Georges Terrace. This was the city they'd been offered, and had accepted. They were safe here, but even now, at rush hour, the wide streets felt empty. That was the bargain. He'd left his city and would never return.

How short-lived gratitude was!

It was like this. Budapest was the glamorous love of his life who had betrayed him. Perth was a flat-faced, wide-hipped country girl whom he'd been forced to take as a wife. Only time would tell if one day he would reach across and take her hand . . .

He had a suspicion that never again would he feel at home as he once had. Never again on this earth. And another suspicion: that to love a place, to imagine yourself belonging to it, was a lie, a fiction: It was a vanity.

Especially for a Jew.

If he didn't know better about human nature – his education had been swift and irrevocable – he would say there was an innocence about this city. Nobody here could imagine the waters of the Swan running red. The Causeway bombed, tanks rolling up St Georges Terrace. Block after block of empty buildings, blackened and broken like ruined teeth. Shots ringing out. The hunted running through Kings Park. Bodies piled ten high on the steps of Parliament House . . . In an eye flash he saw his brother Janos pressed between other bodies, stacked up like firewood against the wall of a slaughterhouse. Janos no longer and yet, as Meyer stood there staring, for one moment, suddenly, vividly, Janos . . .

With a practised movement, Meyer blinked and turned his head.

Strange, in memory it was as if there had always been a shadow haloed behind each one of them, the murdered, like something paranormal caught in a photograph. As if they were marked out, even as children. He didn't know now if he had always sensed this, or added it himself in retrospect.

He, Ida and Frank had left behind all their family and friends, those who had survived. But the dead came with you.

Suddenly he had a yearning to see Frank. He'd nearly reached the railway line, but now, instead of crossing at the Barrack Street Bridge and heading home, he turned left into Wellington Street and started walking up the hill towards West Perth. The sun was sinking, just beneath eye-level.

By the time he reached the Golden Age, the children would have eaten their evening meal, though he did not think they would be sleeping. There were rules about visiting, but Meyer never paid any attention to them.

Nobody now, apart from immigration officials, could stop Meyer from doing anything. He knew this about himself. It was as if there were a little invisible circle around him. He'd noticed this about some men when he was a boy.

This power came from a lack of respect for all that called itself authority.

Not that these days there was anything much he wanted to do.

Still, because of this resolve to see his son, Meyer felt his spirits rise. Small things give you happiness. He'd learnt that, above all else. In the labour camp, a smoke, a starry night, a thicker piece of bread could make them briefly happy as children.

Was all happiness just a memory of childhood?

Meyer paused for a moment by the kerb and lifted his hat to cool his head. It was a treeless road lined by offices, a government department, a warehouse. He would have liked to stop somewhere and have a drink. A chilled white wine in a café with open windows: that didn't exist here. Or even a glass of cold Australian beer. But he knew by the instinct that had always saved him that the bars in the pubs, where the growl of men's voices rose to Babel proportions before six o'clock closing, were no place for a lone New Australian.

He passed other workers on their way home, heads down in the heat and brightness. The men with sun-worn faces, in shirtsleeves and dusty trilbies, the women with freckly arms and buckety white bags and hats, and pointy brassieres.

People grew old quickly here. They had a self-consciousness about them, like country people come to the city.

The city was not small, but there were so few people on the streets. He never saw anyone he knew. In the streets where he'd grown up, at every turn he would see familiar faces, old teachers, former neighbours, ex-classmates and lovers. For him this was a city with no past.

Because of the necessity of being positive and optimistic when he was with Ida, as buoyant as a balloon that must keep them both aloft above some vast open sea that terrified her, it was when he was alone that he became aware of how much he thought about this exile, this new chapter in their life, which was likely to be the last.

Funny, in the beginning, like all lovers, he and Ida were always trying to be alone. Now he enjoyed her best in company. With others, he saw what an accomplished entertainer she was, and how this was – especially if she played the piano – her escape. And therefore his.

At the top of the hill he turned right into Thomas Street and walked past Perth Modern School, the famous state high school. A hallowed place, alma mater to prime ministers, labour leaders, athletes, scholars, scientists, musicians. The sight of its tall trees and dark buildings made him catch his breath for a moment. Frank, who could not speak a word of English when they'd come here, six years later won a scholarship to Modern School. Their little family was stunned by this good news. Then, for the first time since stepping ashore here, they gave themselves to joy. They'd whooped and danced and drunk homemade grappa with the Zanettis next door and sent Frank off to buy fish and chips, the only local food they liked. At last their decision to migrate seemed justified. It was redemption for all the strangeness, low status and disappointments. The son had brought honour to the family! He would have the chance to excel here.

Later they wondered if he could have caught polio queuing up in the fish and chip shop.

Who knew if he would ever go to Modern School now?

Meyer crossed the Thomas Street Bridge and walked up Loftus Street. The sky was apricot-coloured, it would be hot again tomorrow. He had at last learnt to read this city's weather. Just from standing each morning and night in his garden, and exchanging words with old man Vito next door. Vito was a man of the soil.

He turned left into Harrogate Street and saw black birds perched on the chimneys of the Golden Age. For a few minutes after sundown the air here was like clear water. He looked at his watch. His walk had taken him thirty-seven minutes.

The Netting Factory was aglow in the evening sky, but the Golden Age loomed shadowy and silent. He walked through the open door into the twilit hallway with its empty waiting pews, past the Sister's office, into the half-dark corridor. Down in the kitchen there was light and the faint clatter of dishes. Upstairs, distant voices: the nurses having their evening meal. He turned left down the corridor to the Boys Ward and stood in the doorway. A model hospital scene: all the young patients in their beds, neat, washed, with just enough light for them to occupy themselves.

Frank's bed was closest to the door. He was lying up against two pillows, reading a book. His skin had the softness of a child after a bath, and his damp hair was combed back like a little man's. He looked touchingly young, almost babyish, and absurdly like Ida. The book was called *One Thousand and One Nights*. He was reading it the way Ida read, intently, slightly frowning. Absent-mindedly he rotated a finger in one nostril.

His eyes suddenly lifted towards Meyer. A smile of such delight spread across his face that Meyer had the sense of a light coming on.

Meyer sat down humbly on the white cover, next to his son's wasted legs. He felt the blessedness of receiving unconditional affection. It was balm, it soothed him, made his head go quiet at last. This is why the human race goes on having children, he thought. To remind us of the bliss of being loved.

'Why have you come?'

'To see you. I was walking home from work and I thought *vot da hell.*'

Frank laughed like a little child, with an open mouth.

For most of Frank's early life, during the war, Meyer never saw him. Ever since, it had been a continual process of getting to know each other. They were unalike in every way, yet with mutual goodwill had forged a bond, with no need to explain themselves. Neither had ever hurt or bothered the other. Between them was a faint, unstated pact to protect themselves from Ida.

'So, Feri, how are you?'

With Meyer, you did not complain. Unless a problem was presented as something to be solved, it was as if he didn't hear you.

'Today,' Frank said brightly, 'I took two – no, three – steps, on my own.'

It was an offering, Meyer knew, a gift to him. He reached across and took Frank's hand. 'I didn't know you'd started

91

walking.' Better not to make too much of it. The boy often lied.

'I'll play football one day!' There was something false, conventional about this. Someone had suggested it to him. An Australian. Neither he nor Frank had ever taken the slightest interest in football. He could feel the slender bones of Frank's fingers. Not with hands like that, you won't, he thought. Not with those poor little legs clamped between two sticks.

'You'll do everything you really want,' Meyer said. 'You'll see.'

Of all the trials, this one had come closest to bringing Meyer down, though Frank would never know it. As if a curse had pursued them from the Old World and was not quite done with them, still had the cruellest trick of all up its sleeve. It completed his sense of failure, powerlessness that he had not protected his boy.

He was eternally glad that his own father had died in '38, before he could know the fate of his sons. Meyer reached out for the glass of water on the bedside locker. 'May I?'

Frank watched his father's Adam's apple moving rapidly up and down as he drained the glass. He was thirsty, he must have walked a long way to come here.

Meyer picked up Frank's book. 'Do you like this?'

'Yes. I'm reading a story called "Aladdin".'

'I read it once, in Hungarian.'

'I like the magic lamp and the genie. And the flying carpets!'

'I'd like a ride home now on one of those carpets. Your mother is waiting for me. You know her, she will be worried.'

Meyer stood up and looked down at Frank, remote as a monument, with his lean face, broken nose and dark wavy hair. His eyes had twinkles of sadness in them, like leftover tears. Beneath his gaze, Frank felt suddenly very small and weak. *Apuci*. Daddy. The quiet giant in his landscape. He wanted to whine 'Don't go!' like some of the other kids did to their parents. That was out of the question with Meyer.

His father bent down and kissed him.

He didn't look like a young child now, Meyer thought, as he turned to wave from the doorway. Frank was lying back on his pillows staring into space. His eyes were serious, his cheeks sunken and his mouth had the faintly bitter resolve of a much older person.

Meyer knew Frank loved him intensely. As Ida did. As had his parents and his brothers and his one poor little sister, Roszi, and his friends, nearly all of whom had died in the war. Wherever he went he carried their love around with him, their mysterious, unasked-for gift, like a bundle on a stick over his shoulder.

He sometimes thought he only loved properly in retrospect.

He'd often wondered whether he had a cooler temperament than others, and that was why he had survived.

Since the war he'd been unable to say goodbye to anyone. Couldn't bring himself to say the word, in any language. Nor would he ever say 'See you soon.'

He couldn't unlearn the practice of death, living with the closeness of its presence, like a roar in his ears. Like a sailor keeps hearing the sea.

Frank, staring from his pillows at the high dark window opposite, was engaged in composing a poem.

Return to the road, father!
Into the dark.
I rub my lamp
But you don't come back.

He took the prescription pad out of the pocket of his dressing gown. Then suddenly he threw off his covers and reached for the wheelchair. There was something he wanted to tell his father. That he was a poet!

A woman was coming down the stairs as Meyer walked past.

'Mr Gold!'

He turned. It was Sister Penny descending in high heels, all bright-haired in a jade-green brocade dress with a shiny brooch pinned where her watch usually was, above her left breast. From here he had a full view of her legs. In high heels her calves were strong and rounded, her ankles long and slim like a pair of inverted bottles. She carried a beaded bag hanging on a gold chain from her arm and a pair of white gloves in her hand.

'Goodness, it's dark down here!' She reached the bottom step and turned on a switch. 'It's such a lovely evening. We were eating dinner on the balcony and couldn't drag ourselves away.' They stood blinking at each other in the institutional light, bathed in the faintly oriental aura of her perfume.

'Is everything all right, Mr Gold?'

'Thank you, yes. I was passing and had a sudden vish to tell my son goodnight.'

An instant smile, pure, generous, without authority, lit up Sister Penny's face. 'That would have made him so very happy.'

No frown, no mention of rules or visiting hours.

'It's my night off,' she said, as they walked together down the hall, her high heels clicking on the floor. 'I'm going to a play at my daughter's college.' She was smiling, very pleased.

'Is your daughter an actor in the play?'

'Oh no, Elizabeth Ann is very reserved. She's taking tickets at the door.'

Funny, he found her more attractive, more extraordinary, in uniform rather than like this, outfitted according to the rather matronly rules of style of Australian women. To him they all looked a little like servants dressed up, or big school-girls. He felt more at ease with her in uniform, and in the official, matter-of-factness of their exchange. Now it was necessary to make conversation. He didn't know quite what to say.

'How is my son?' he asked, as they approached the front door.

'He's making good progress.'

'He told me he is walking now.'

'Did he? That hasn't been reported to me yet.' A small, humorous smile appeared on her face for a moment. 'But he's certainly well on the way.'

'I see.' So she knew Frank could be inventive with the truth.

She turned to him. 'You know, the children are aware of how worried their parents are. They try to cheer them up, they really do.'

The last light of the day fell in low streaks down the hall. He could see the flesh-pink powder on her nose and the red grease across her lips. For a moment her face was a mask and only her eyes were true, dark with a secret life, a knowledge.

'Sometimes a little storytelling keeps us going,' she said.

'You mean lying?'

She laughed with her head thrown back. How happy she is, he thought. A widow. Who is her lover?

'I must be off.' She adjusted her bag on her arm and smiled at him. 'Elizabeth Ann would never forgive me if I was late.' He stood back for her to pass through the door.

On the verandah a woman came running towards them, a dumpy, untidy figure who seemed to be in a state of panic, everything coming apart, blouse straining over heavy breasts, bare legs shoved into ugly shoes, short thick hair unbrushed like a little kid's.

'*Roszi*!' Meyer murmured. A shiver ran down his spine.

'Goodness, all the parents are turning up tonight!' said Sister Penny.

'Oh, Sister!' the woman cried. Her face was red, about to crumble into tears. 'I got a lift with a neighbour! I know it's after-hours, but I haven't seen Elsa for so long . . .'

'Go right on in, Mrs Briggs. There's still a few minutes before lights out.'

Without a word, the woman ducked past them and ran through the front door.

Frank, too late, came rolling out of Boys to catch Meyer before he left, and nearly bowled over Elsa's mother.

They said nothing as they crossed the verandah. Sister Penny's little pale blue Morris Minor was parked on the road.

She hesitated. 'I can offer you a lift, if you're going my way.'

Meyer indicated the other direction. 'I'm going to the station.'

'Goodnight then, Mr Gold.'

He bowed. 'Enjoy your evening.'

'I will!'

Their eyes agreed to disengage.

Why as he walked away did everything feel different? The velvety dusk, the lights appearing, the pencilled clarity of roofs and trees. Softening, the city seemed more grown up, more itself, with its own mystery and potential. He was starting to see it differently, to look a little kindly upon it, as if, without knowing, bit by bit it had been taking shape for him. As if the disappointments and resentments had begun to evaporate into this silken air . . . A desert town, isolated, provincial, slowly gaining depth and shade, a mythic city too, in its own way. For the first time he felt a return to a certain lightness, a shadow of the way in which he had once lived on the streets of Budapest.

This nurse was not a conventional person. Like him, she had come to her own conclusions. She was vibrant with life and yet she was solitary. Unburdened by domesticity. She was brave, even audacious. Kept her disappointments in their place. How had a woman like that come to live alone? All this, standing at the bottom of the stairs, he had known in a glance.

There was a call between them, clear as a bird's, so that you looked up at once to trace it. They recognised each other.

Back there on the road, in the fairground lights of the Netting Factory, they had taken each other's measure. And decided to turn their backs.

All the same, he remembered the sensation when they parted, the tiny gap where something was needed, when the most natural thing in the world would have been the way of a man and woman parting, a kiss, an embrace. A salute.

He had a feeling of escape.

Something had been taken away from him in the war, against his will, and he would never be the same. Years in labour camps, in mountains, in salt mines: only solitude was natural to him now. Some part of him was terminally tired. He was beyond intimacy. The pretence at normality, the weight of the past, the unreality of the days here had exhausted him.

Just as the train came crashing out of the darkness into Leederville station, he had a sudden memory of the time, soon after their arrival in Perth, that he, Ida and Frank had walked from the Migrant Hostel to Swanbourne Beach. They'd run down through giant sandhills, across the vast white sand and stood gazing at the Indian Ocean that stretched all the way to Africa. It was winter, they were the only people there. Ida and Frank took off their shoes and ran along the shore, playing tag with the waves. He, tired from carrying Frank for the last mile on his shoulders, lay back on the sand in the middle of the beach with his eyes closed.

The Antipodes, he had thought. The bottom of the world. All he could hear was the roar of the surf, the crack of the waves breaking, the call of circling birds. How could his heavy soul bear such endlessness? Such loneliness. He caught the sound of Frank and Ida laughing, screaming in the wind.

Such wildness and freedom.

Such peace.

Lie down with me.

Where did those words come from?

14.

Margaret in Her Garden

All day long the desert easterly blew through the suburb, and by sundown, though the wind had dropped, the air hung hot and close in the house. Margaret left the baby on the rug in the shadowy lounge room, where Sally lay sprawled on the couch. Fat Jane smiled in her chins and waved her chunky arms, but Sally was listening to *The Argonauts* on the wireless. She wasn't as helpful with Jane as Elsa had been. In fact, ever since she'd had to take on Elsa's tasks, Sally had been in a bad mood.

Oh the relief to open the back door, stand on the wooden steps and disappear into those green shades! The grapevine tendrils heaped over the trellis, the old fig by the washhouse, the thick rustling line of neighbours' trees above the fences: all so familiar to her it was as if they had faces. Beyond the clothesline the wild oats rippled across their yard like a field of wheat. No one had the energy this year to pull them out. Nor to pick the rotten figs, black dripping pouches haloed by midges.

Everything was quiet. It was too hot for the birds' end-of-day chorus. All the neighbourhood children were inside. Even the ants had disappeared. It was the start of a heatwave, she could feel it, a stillness like an animal lying in wait. The first of the summer, and no sea breeze as yet. Margaret set the sprinkler on the little scratchy stretch of grass.

At this time of the day she always found an excuse to go outside for a moment. It was as if she was being called. If she didn't go she felt trapped.

Once, long ago, when she was fifteen and working in the post-office store at a crossroads two hundred miles south of Perth, after closing up at six she used to walk through the Flats, a forest of dead trees that stretched out behind the shop as far as she could see. There was nowhere else to go. It was a poor thing, like her, yet over the months, as she made her way across its cracked mud tiles, the slime never far below, she started to feel its presence, its gentleness and endurance. It was host to a family of wild creatures, frogs, birds, snakes. The light through the stark branches was delicate, consoling. It was never silent there and she did not feel alone.

It had been hot like this nine months ago, when she'd come home at midday one Saturday from shopping in the city and seen the ambulance in their driveway. From that time on, her body has been in the grip of something, heavy as a stone in her belly, pulling down her mouth and neck and shoulders. Sometimes the garden was the only place where she could breathe. Night after night when Elsa was in Isolation, she paced up and down the little stretch of grass.

The garden told her things.

That first day, when she and Jack had returned from the hospital and all they could do was wait, a black crow flew out of the twilight and knocked a slender bone against the trunk of the fig tree. Tap-tap-tap, like the spirit of cruel Nature sending her a message – *This is it! This is it!* – until Margaret ran inside.

Nance had driven over with a casserole and questioned Margaret about hygiene. Did she let her girls use public conveniences? Did she check if they washed their hands? Margaret opened her mouth and screamed. Even Jack thought Nance had overstepped. He put his arm around Margaret, but she ran outside again, into the darkness beyond the washing line. She couldn't bear the presence of people any more.

She lay down in the grass and the moon went higher. The stars tumbled across the black bowl of the sky and the grasses rustled around her. She heard the shiftings of tiny creatures in the earth and the drone of midges. Everything was in motion. Minute by minute the backyard was reverting to wildness. She felt she was lying on the heart of a great animal. It was asking for her trust. All she could do was trust.

Somewhere, a long time ago, she'd found this out, and then forgotten. Making soup, washing nappies, she had turned her back on the springs of life. Never again would she do this, never, ever! If Elsa lived . . .

The sun had just sunk when through the gap in the pickets she saw Raymond Hoffman's truck parked in his mother's driveway. Raymond usually called in for a cup of tea on the way from his farm, with a truckload of fruit and vegetables for the markets.

The markets were in West Perth. Not far from the Golden Age.

Margaret, without another thought, stepped through the gap in the fence, ran across Ada Hoffman's vast bare yard and up the steep back steps to her verandah. Ada's pet sheep lay under the steps as if it were dead.

'Yoo-hoo!' Shy Margaret boldly sang out the neighbourhood call through the flywire of the door. Raymond and Ada Hoffman were sitting at the kitchen table, solid figures with a pot of tea between them. They turned their grey-blue, sceptical North of England eyes on Margaret. Through the flywire, gabbling a little, she asked Raymond for a lift to visit Elsa. Ada waved her inside.

'I haven't seen her for so long,' Margaret said, standing in the doorway clutching her apron. 'The baby's been sick.' To her surprise she heard her voice wobbling. Not just from sorrow, as they would think, but also from anger.

This morning in the bathroom she'd stood behind Jack as he was shaving and said, 'I'm looking forward to the Golden Age this Sunday.'

'Not on, I'm afraid,' Jack said, lifting his chin to scrape so his voice went strained. 'I promised Nance I'd fix her fence. She's made all the arrangements.'

'But I haven't seen Elsa for three weeks!'

'You know I have,' Jack said irritably. 'You know she's all right.'

He was bad-tempered because he knew what she didn't need to say to him, that he always did his sister's bidding. Nance! Nance had been to see Elsa with Jack while she stayed home with a sick baby! She wanted to grind her teeth, stamp her feet, throw something.

The Hoffmans, Ada and Raymond, sat stolidly in the twilight at the kitchen table. They both had large-lobed ears and strong-featured faces with long, tanned, fine-skinned fleshy cheeks, like toby jugs. They didn't say anything. This was the effect polio had on people, Margaret knew. They went silent. It was like traffic stopping for an ambulance to pass. In this silence Margaret had learnt to press on, to ask for what she needed. A pound of stewing steak, please. A dozen eggs. *What's the matter? Frightened I'm going to breathe on you . . . ?*

When Margaret and Jack came home from Perth that Saturday, the ambulance they saw in their driveway had been called by Ada. She took Sally and Jane home with her that night. Ada was a woman of few words, but she'd stood by the Briggs.

Most people now seemed very far from Margaret, but Ada had stayed the same.

Raymond made a noise in his throat and indicated his cup of tea.

'I'll be ready in five minutes,' Margaret said, hardly believing her own daring. Jack would be home soon to help Sally. They could manage without her for once.

The truck was too noisy for conversation. Two shy people could sit on the rattling seats high up above the evening traffic, lost in their own thoughts. Now that she was on her way to Elsa, all her lethargy, anxiety and anger had disappeared. She sat up straight, alert to everything, the farm smells of the truck, petrol, hay, manure, Raymond's square brown hands on the wheel. A bachelor farmer. She knew the type from her time at the Flats. The sun was setting behind them. Everything was flowing, smooth as water. How would

103

it be to live like this, lightly, following your heart, as if her life were not a heavy ship she struggled to keep on course?

She'd withdrawn from contact with most people. She sent Sally to the shops when she could. The first time she'd walked into the butcher's after Elsa went to hospital, some people walked out.

It seemed to her now that her home had a darkness about it, a mark on its door. She felt like an outcast when she pushed her pram up the road past the other houses.

Prayers had been offered at church for Elsa, but the only place Margaret prayed now was outside, alone, at night. She prayed to lose her anger with Reverend Hollis for not turning up when she'd asked him to bless Elsa in the Isolation Ward. *His war leg playing up.* She prayed to forgive him. He had children of his own. But what did it say about his faith?

Elsa had got better by herself.

The truck moved ponderously, the slowest vehicle on the road. The evening star appeared. Margaret, afraid of regulations, prayed that she'd reach Elsa before lights out.

Elsa was reading, *Anne of Green Gables*, when she heard the clopping sound of her mother's shoes, and suddenly there was Margaret's face, red, shining like a moon, bearing down on her, eyes bright with happiness and expectation. Elsa sensed that her mother wanted to embrace her and she found herself drawing back.

'How'd you get here?'

'In Raymond Hoffman's truck.'

'What about Jane?'

'I left her with Sally. Dad'll be home by now.'

'What's he going to say?'

Their eyes locked for a moment. Elsa patted a spot next to her legs.

Margaret sank down and, sighing with relief, wriggled her large soft rear backwards in a confiding, proprietary way. Her eyes travelled around the high ceiling of the room. The little girls in the other beds politely read their books.

'Where are all the nurses?' Margaret asked.

'Upstairs. Having their tea.'

'A boy in the corridor said there was time to see you. Pale lad, pointy face.'

'Frank Gold. He's new.' But already he was everywhere, knew everything, Elsa thought. What was he doing out of bed?

'It was a spur-of-the-moment decision, love. I came just as I was!'

For a moment Elsa felt as if she were looking at her mother through the wrong end of a telescope. Seeing from far away the face of her childhood, the hook nose, the soft, furry face, the broken capillaries. The eyes like crushed blue flowers.

Margaret was too happy to care how she looked. Her shiny white shins sprinkled with sparse hairs stuck out as she sat back on the bed, her old shoes dangling. Her thick black hair, barbered short, sprang out around her head. The front of her dress was stained.

Elsa fought off a sense of invasion. This was her favourite time of the day, reading before lights out. She felt calm, weightless, no part of her as yet cramped or in pain. It was a smooth time, everyone at peace. The Netting Factory's glow filled the windows. The pages of her book came alive and filled her head with other lives as she fell asleep.

'This is a good place,' Margaret said. They often picked up each other's thoughts. 'Daddy said you've started walking.'

'A bit, with crutches.'

Talking wasn't the point when you were with Margaret. Her mother didn't ask many questions. She knew how you were by being with you. Often she brought a treat, a red apple, a bunch of muscat grapes, her favourites, which she fed you one by one. She was always close, part of you, like a mother animal. Slowly that heat was reaching Elsa. She started to relax, a yawning, cranky little cub again.

'It's tiring you.'

'What is?'

'This walking.'

'Mum, it's what I'm here for!' Elsa was annoyed because her mother was right. Walking was so ferociously hard that she feared she would give up, be one of those who didn't make it. This fear shadowed her.

Margaret grieved that her daughter had to carry this burden. Elsa, each time she saw her, had become more adult. She had lost her childhood. If she didn't see Elsa more often, didn't pay her close attention, Margaret wouldn't keep up with her. Her daughter would outgrow her.

'I couldn't come before, love. Jane wouldn't stay with anyone but me.'

'It doesn't matter, Mum.' It *really* didn't but it would hurt her mother if she said this too emphatically.

The nurses were coming down the stairs in a wave of footsteps and laughter. In a moment they would burst in with their bright, happy faces, and whisk from bed to bed. It happened very fast. Her mother would be in the way.

It was as if she had changed sides and belonged here now.

Margaret jumped up and started hunting for her bag. She knew that Elsa wanted her to leave.

'It's all right, Mum! They won't punish you!'

Margaret bent down to kiss her. She was never angry with her children. For her they were always right.

Elsa's irritation faded with the echo of Margaret's footsteps down the corridor. Her shoes clattered because they were too big. She'd bought a size up, on sale, and stuffed paper in the toes.

What her mother had to get used to was that it was she, Elsa, who had to deal with what had happened to her. Margaret and all the rest of them would only hold her back.

But she could never forget the knowledge that had come to her when she woke up in Isolation and her fever had gone. She knew she'd only kept breathing because of her mother. So that her mother wouldn't die.

Margaret searched the night sky for the moon as she trudged to the station. It was to her left, a sliver hanging somewhere over her own roof. Now to prepare the case for the defence, she thought. This time her absence had been so reckless, so out of line, there was no point in making an excuse. Jack would look at her as if she were a crazy woman, his lips tight with the burden of her. When he told her she was crazy it always made her cry. He didn't have to say it any more.

There were so many reasons for everything that she could never begin to explain. Because everything was joined up, like the nursery rhyme. *For want of a nail, the shoe was lost.*

It was very simple really. 'I had to go, love,' she would say. Before the horse was lost, the rider was lost, before, without Elsa, the whole family fell apart.

Leave it at that. 'I feel better now,' she would say.

Perhaps he'd be glad for her.

She tried to hide it, what Elsa was for her. Sally always said that Elsa was the favourite, though Margaret knew she loved them all the same. But Elsa was the first. Elsa had borne the full force of the fear and clumsiness and wonder of new parents. They had grown up together.

Ever since Elsa fell sick, Jack had been so bad-tempered that lots of nights Margaret got up when he was snoring and went to Elsa's bed in the girls' room. Lay for hours looking at the dark sky moving past the window.

When she was first married, she went to tell her father in the Old Men's Home. Once she was grown up, and had a job, he'd sometimes turn up to see her and ask to borrow money. Now, without his teeth but with perfect authority, as if he himself had been an ideal husband and father, he said, 'I hope he's easygoing. Never marry a bad-tempered man, Marge.'

'I have, Pa,' she said. Her father was the only person in the world she could say this to. She laughed. Didn't care two hoots what he thought. She was newly pregnant and deliri-ously cheerful.

Elsa was the compensation for everything. From the moment she was put in Margaret's arms, it was as if the stars came out. She knew at once this child was special. So graceful and dignified that people seemed to bow before her in her pram! This was the best thing that had ever happened to Margaret. The turning point. Her life had at last been made right.

The shock and violence of polio, the instant transforma-tion of it, reminded her of a cruel trick, of sorcery in a fairytale. As if an evil monster had demanded the fairest in the land. Elsa was the sacrifice.

Sometimes now, when she was alone, Margaret felt her own hand curl over, and let her hip lurch and swivel a little as she walked.

For some reason she thought about the bird she had seen last week when she was hanging out the wash. She'd become aware of it standing a few feet away, watching her. When she crouched down, it stood its ground, quivering, its eyes outraged, astonished. Proud but asking for her help. The centre of its pale grey chest was split open and a spill of downy grey and white feathers were piled upon the ground. Suddenly, laboriously, it raised its wings and disappeared into the wilderness of backyards.

Frank asked the nurse on night duty, the one called Hadley Dent, if he could go to the toilet.

'Would a bottle do?'

'No. I've undone my splints.'

'Be quick then.'

He wheeled straight to the open door of Girls and hissed through the crack between the hinges, 'Was that your mother?' He felt bolder after seeing Meyer. *Vot da hell!*

'Yes.'

'She doesn't look like you.' Elsa's mother looked like a cleaning lady or a washerwoman. Her daughter was a beautiful wildflower, springing up in a field of cabbages . . .

Elsa didn't answer. She wasn't in a talking mood.

'Oh well. G'night.'

'See you tomorrow,' Elsa said.

'Naturally,' said Frank, in his suavest tone. To his horror, his voice scraped and squeaked. It wasn't till he was back in bed that he was able to give himself to it. 'See you tomorrow.' It was what friends said! Acknowledgement! Of what?

That they belonged to no one but themselves.

15.

Christmas

On Christmas Day all the city children went home except for Frank, whose parents had volunteered to serve lunch and wash up at the Golden Age so that Nella and the local nurses could spend the day with their families. As the Golds explained to the children, their religion did not celebrate Christmas and they did not have family here (nor anywhere else in the world, which they did not say). They were helped by two nurses, Ngaire from New Zealand, and Hadley Dent from England. Even Norm Whitehouse, a bachelor, who lived in a rooming house two streets away, had a married niece who'd invited him for lunch.

Frank was apprehensive about this exposure, the invasion of one world by another. He felt uneasy, as if Ida and Meyer might break into Hungarian songs, or reveal their critical attitudes to Australia, or their un-Australian fits of passion or melancholy, or serve up something foreign, like pickled fish, and smoke too many cigarettes.

He wished Elsa had stayed so his parents could meet her – they were always appreciative of beauty. He would have liked to see if they understood her special quality. But Elsa had left at nine in the morning in a pale-blue Morris Minor, driven by a woman with white hair, whom he presumed was her Auntie Nance. Her father had jumped out of the passenger's seat and come to fetch Elsa.

Frank watched from the verandah as she slowly made her way on crutches across Alfred Street, her father hovering in case she fell. That would annoy her. Frank knew Elsa's pride and determination, but her family knew only pity. He felt an ache for her, as he watched her enter the car in the way they had practised countless times with Lidja, bottom first in the passenger's seat, then picking up the legs and swivelling. As usual, every movement Elsa made had grace.

It was only as her father was fitting her crutches into the boot that Frank noticed a smaller girl in the back seat. Unsmiling, looking straight ahead, she had pale skin and ginger hair in plaits. She did not lean forward to say hello, nor did Elsa turn to greet her. That must be Sally, the sister she never talked about. A chill ran up Frank's spine. These days he and Elsa had fallen into the habit of telling each other about everyone in their lives, but there was a silence around Sally. Nance got out to let Jack Briggs climb into the back seat next to Sally. He sat with his head forward, too large for his sister's car. Elsa looked steadily ahead.

Frank made his way back to the kitchen, where he saw his mother putting on Nella's apron.

'What?' he heard Warren Barrett say to Meyer, who was hanging up balloons above the long wooden table. 'Don't you believe in Jesus?'

Frank left the room.

But the Golden Age Christmas turned out well. They pulled crackers and Meyer read out the jokes on the little slips of paper in an exaggerated foreign accent which made them laugh. They all wore paper crowns – even Ida, balanced askew above her haughty face – and it had a democratising effect. The children looked like little royals and the adults looked as pitiful as clowns. The country babies, Rayma and Denise, were passed from lap to lap.

This is the community we belong to now, Meyer thought. With the humble of the earth. The halt and the lame.

He carved the turkey which Ida, following Nella's instructions, had watched over, and played the French waiter with a white serviette over his arm. None of the children, except for Frank, knew what a French waiter was, but they laughed their heads off because they knew it was a game. And all children, everywhere, love a game.

Since she was religious, and on duty, Hadley would not take even a sip of the sweet wine Meyer poured, but Ngaire had a glass and grew quite flushed. Norm Whitehouse returned early with his pockets full of sweets. Ida played the piano and they sang 'Silent Night' and 'Jingle Bells' and 'God Save the Queen'.

Sister Olive Penny also returned early. She'd invited her daughter to lunch at the Palace Hotel, but Elizabeth Ann

113

wished to spend Christmas at home with her friend Gillian Budd's family, with whom she boarded. You can come too, if you want, Elizabeth Ann told her mother. Gillian's mother had taken Elizabeth Ann aside to tell her she could ask Olive.

By the time Olive made her way up the long pathway across the Budds's green lawn, Elizabeth Ann had opened the front door. She was smiling. The night before, she had sung a solo in the midnight carol service. Olive had never seen her quiet little daughter so happy, so sure of herself. There were many family jokes that Olive could not keep track of as she sipped her thimble glass of sherry. A family pleased with itself, she thought, a success. All that Elizabeth Ann had ever wanted. Olive sat quite silent, unaddressed, with her fine legs crossed in their best nylons and her paper crown slipping low over her too bright, too youthful hair. She took the damned thing off.

Across the table Elizabeth Ann's eyes were brilliant as her diamond chips. The air shimmered a little between her and the eldest son of the house, Olive picked that up at once. Timothy. Tim Budd. So much in the eldest brother role of chief tease and joker, it was impossible to know what he was like. A high-coloured, smooth face, hair side-parted, combed back, college style. Eyes that didn't see Olive, she wasn't part of his world.

After the pudding and brandy sauce had been eaten, she murmured about short-staffing at the hospital and excused herself. Elizabeth Ann gave her a wide smile and a charming wave when she left, but did not see her off. Tim had come to sit next to her.

As soon as Olive walked into the Golden Age kitchen, Meyer poured a glass of sweet wine called Tokay for her.

It was a relief to see his face. Why? A face without innocence, without complacency. With the back of her hand she rubbed the cheek of Susan Bennett, whose parents had cut short their Christmas lunch together – they'd been invited to a party on a ship, Ngaire muttered – and sat down with Julia Snow on one knee and Lucy Boyer on the other.

'You are home,' Meyer said.

Nothing escapes him, she thought.

Love seemed to shine at her from every pair of eyes. Her own eyes prickled. What was this Hungarian wine? Its warmth seeped through her. She had another glass.

Just before the children were put to bed, Ida went to the schoolroom piano and played a little of Mozart's '*Ah vous dirai-je, Maman*'. At once they all wanted to sing. Of course! It was the nursery tune, 'Twinkle Twinkle, Little Star'. Even the babies jigged. A couple of tears ran down Hadley's fresh pink-and-white face. Homesick, she supposed. For the Lakes, for her own golden-green childhood.

Frank felt it as a relief. When his mother was at the piano she was distant from him. For once she took her eyes off him. But as a little kid, apparently he used to climb up on her knee to stop her. Now he liked to watch her, on her own, not anxious or angry, not needing anything. Somehow he knew that what she did was very good. In this role he had respect for her, and gratitude. It seemed to justify everything, their foreignness, their victimhood in the other country. It brought honour to them. He wished that Elsa was there to hear her.

'Poor girl,' Meyer thought, watching Ida. 'Poor girl.' He saw her mouth relaxed, in charge, that bitter little mouth that usually gripped a cigarette. How long since she had played for other people? He hadn't heard the piano since Frank fell ill.

To Meyer, the music, its plangent song of childhood, seemed like an elegy. For all the children caught in this plague. For the parents he'd passed, not so long ago, as they left Princess Margaret Hospital, weeping, the mother clutching a teddy bear.

Sister Penny stayed very still. She never listened to music, never sat down for relaxation, only laid her head on her pillow last thing at night. Since coming to live at the Golden Age, she didn't even turn on the wireless – someone was always trying to sleep. If asked she'd say she liked dance music, tango, 'Perfidia', 'With a Song in My Heart' – something you moved to. She was startled by Ida's ease and precision. Her concentration, her accuracy, reminded Olive of the skills that were her personal exultation, of a good surgeon at work, or nurses laying out a body. Her own deftness and judgement.

Ida finished the piece, let her hands fall into her lap, her head bowed. Olive, clapping, remembered that Frank had spoken of his mother playing the piano. She hadn't really taken it in. A lot of people had a go at playing the piano. But now she knew that Frank's mother was a professional.

Because Olive was used to connecting emotions to practical results, she thought: *Concert.* A fundraiser. The Golden Age's celebration of the impending royal visit! *The Queen's Concert.* She saw the poster. *'Tickets, One Pound. Five Shillings Concession.'*

The children who celebrated Christmas at the Golden Age seemed much happier than those who returned at bedtime, exhausted, silent, distant and alone.

Elsa was pale with dark rings under her eyes. Without greeting anybody, she went straight to her bed. Frank felt an

116

irrational gratification. As if she had found out she belonged here now, with him, not back with her family.

Until they went home they'd forgotten they were in a tragedy. Old haunts, toys, books lay all around them, remnants of a past life. Other siblings had taken over their bikes, their beds, their place in the family. Some families treated them like babies, almost needing to be fed. Others, like Malcolm Poole's father, expected more progress. There was an ugly scene when Malcolm, returning to Boys, too tired to speak, lay down straight away on his bed.

'On your feet, my lad!' his father hissed, as if at the end of his patience. 'Stand up when you say goodbye to me! Shake hands . . . that's the way. A little more grit needed now . . . Time you were walking, my boy!'

Silence fell over Boys. Malcolm lay down again, unable to move any limb at all. Mr Poole walked out, his hands clenching and unclenching, his crepe soles squeaking over the polished boards. For the rest of the night, no sound came from Malcolm's bed.

Sister Penny popped her head out of the office as Mr Poole walked past and asked if she could have a word. When he left, his head seemed lower in his collar, and for several minutes, while he beat on the steering wheel and his horn blared on and off, his car wouldn't start.

Only little Albert Sutton cried because he didn't want to come back. He was seven years old, the youngest of six children, immigrants from England, the one born in Australia. He cried for his parents and his four brothers and one sister, all of whom accompanied him back to the Golden Age. They stood around his bed, a great crowd, all strong, white-skinned, black-haired.

'Now then, our Albert, tears won't make you better,' said his father.

'You'll be home in no time, love,' his mother said.

But his big sister, Lizzie, in an exact, dramatic movement, swooped on her tiny brother, picked him up and danced him cheek to cheek around the room, humming, serious, as if he were her man. She closed her eyes in a dream, flushed rosy, her long dark hair falling down her back. The watching boys in their beds held their breath. Frank could almost feel her warm cheek on his. A shiver ran through him. It was the same feeling he used to have when he saw his mother's friend, Audrey Singerman. Even when he was quite old, Audrey would sit him on her lap, so close to her that he could feel her breasts and the throb in the soft depth of her body.

'Lizzie's little man,' Frank heard Albert's father say as the brother and sister swirled around the dormitory. 'From the day he were born . . .'

Lizzie laid Albert down on his bed and whispered in his ear. He didn't move. Then, like a flock of birds, the Sutton family rose all together and in a clatter of shoes disappeared out the door. Albert put his pillow over his face to pretend he wasn't there.

'It's always like this,' said Sister Penny, as she thanked the Golds in the hall. 'Christmas is very unsettling.' She personally felt a hollowness about Christmas and had to be brisk with herself. 'Bring on 1954!' she said, smiling at them as she closed the door behind them. When something ends, she thought, something new takes its place. She heard the children's voices rising in the dormitories as they showed off their presents, and she headed into Boys clapping her hands.

Nella, back in her kitchen, was wiping down the benches. The Golds had done a good job, but she needed to put her stamp on it. 'Like a cat lickin' its lair,' Norm Whitehouse said, watching her rearrange the pots and pans. 'Which is the polite way of putting it.' He went to drink his last cup of tea on the step in the doorway.

'Funny the way the stars seem so bright at Christmas,' he called out.

Nella took his cup and rinsed it. 'That's because the Factory lights are out.'

'Are you awake?' Frank whispered through the hinges of the open door to Girls. It was twenty minutes after lights out and still he couldn't sleep. He wasn't used to spending a day without speaking to Elsa. He wanted to find out why she was sad. If she didn't answer him, she was either asleep or didn't feel like talking. It was worth the risk.

'Yes.'

He could just hear her. It wasn't exactly an invitation, but his heart thumped with relief. For where would he go if there was no Elsa? What could he do with all these feelings he carried round? She was his homing point, the place he returned to. His escape, his refuge. His park, his river, his track. Even being parted from her for most of a day made him feel uneasy. He saw now that everything that had ever happened to him led him to her. That everything had turned out *right*.

All these thoughts he'd jotted down in the prescription pad for future reference. Sullivan had said his notes were intended for a sonnet sequence: Frank wasn't sure what form his poem would take, but he knew its title. 'For Elsa'.

Careful to lodge each rubber tip of his crutches firmly on the polished boards, step by step he made his way around the door. She pointed to a place for him to sit, beside her legs, rigid in their splints beneath the sheet.

Frank put his crutches together and leant them up against the end of her bed. He sat. Her head was propped up on her pillow. She wasn't smiling, but her eyes shone at him. Suddenly he knew she'd been waiting for him.

There was something she wanted to tell him.

'You're lucky.'

'Why?'

'You don't have any brothers or sisters.'

Now he was bold enough to do what he'd long planned. He edged himself closer to her, swivelled and half lay back, lifting his weak left leg with his hands onto the bed, followed by his right one. At last he reclined, slowly lowering his head onto the pillow beside hers.

'Why is that lucky?' They lay side by side, in silence, without looking at each other. The back of his hand just grazed hers. His heart pounded.

Staring up at the ceiling, in a low, racing whisper, she told him her onset story.

Every Saturday morning, after she'd turned twelve, Elsa went for a tennis lesson at the Cottesloe Tennis Club. Her father believed it was an important social skill to know how to play tennis.

'To meet the right sort of people,' Frank said. Which he was probably not. He'd spent much of his life in the company of adults and knew how they thought.

Her father worked on Saturday mornings at the bank. Sometimes her mother caught the train with him to go shopping in the city. She left Jane in Elsa's care. When tennis lessons started, Sally had to stay with Jane.

Sally said it wasn't fair. She was the one who loved tennis, who slammed a ball with the family racquet against the shed door for hours on end. Never mind that her turn would come.

One Saturday, the last Saturday of the old life, Elsa couldn't hit the ball. Her arms felt tired, her eyes blurred, her head ached, and even though she knew the lessons cost good money, she asked to be excused. By the time she turned into North Street, she didn't have the strength to ride uphill. It took her a long time to push her bike in the blinding sun and as she turned into their driveway, she collapsed, hitting the side of her head on the earth, one leg trapped beneath the bike, the other hitched up over it.

Sally had been waiting on the porch. She stalked up the driveway, Fat Jane on her hip, and stood over Elsa.

'You're late!'

Elsa did not move.

'It's your turn to mind Jane!' shouted Sally. '*Ged up!*'

She kicked Elsa, two or three sharp nudges on the elbow that was sticking out from under the handlebar, and on the foot caught under the pedal. Jane started to cry. Elsa did not move. '*Gair-dup!*' Sally kept shouting and kicking. By now she too was crying. Jane opened her mouth and screamed.

Elsa felt each kick shudder through her aching body. Something is terribly wrong with me, she thought, and Sally doesn't care.

Suddenly Mrs Hoffman's voice was above her. 'Now then, girls, what's going on here?' She must have pushed her way through the teatree hedge.

Everything went quiet. Elsa felt her arm being gently lifted off the handlebar. She smelt mutton fat. Sometimes she'd watched Mrs Hoffman's large, tanned, greasy hands rolling chops in flour for stew. She felt her leg being raised and the bike sliding away from her. Every movement made her groan.

'Sally, put the baby down and help me get Elsa out of this hot sun.'

Sally and Ada hauled Elsa up and, slinging her arms around their shoulders, half-carried, half-dragged her up the porch steps. The house at midday was coolest in the dining room, in the middle of the house. They laid her on the floor. Elsa turned her head – she wouldn't be able to do this again for several weeks – onto the hearth in front of the unlit gas fire and put her burning cheek upon the cold, shiny green-glazed tiles. There seemed to be tremendous commotion all around her, Sally's voice high-pitched, Jane crying, Mrs Hoffman's heavy shoes clomping up and down the hall. All sounds hurt her. Next thing she heard was the siren of the ambulance.

A thin wail broke out of the nursery. Lying very still, Elsa and Frank listened to the padding footsteps of Ngaire, barefoot, coming downstairs from the Nurses Quarters to take Rayma up to her bed.

Silence descended, and a more serious darkness without, for this one night, the Netting Factory lights. There was nothing more to say. Frank sighed, sat up and slowly slid his legs off the bed. It was like tearing himself in two. He turned towards Elsa, bent his head and quickly kissed her on the lips. Elsa's eyelids closed.

He grasped his crutches and left at once, back to Boys, onto his bed, shivering. He could hardly believe what he had done. So that was how it felt! He reached for his prescription pad.

'I can still feel the touch of your mouth,' he wrote.

Later, still awake, he thought of Sally. He knew her in some way. She was marked. Like a chalk streak across her forehead, she bore the mark of The Unfavourite. How did he know this? Because so often he also was The Unfavourite.

If Sally could, she would call Elsa 'Miss Perfect'. Out of the question now because of polio. In her bedroom Sally probably pursed her lips and talked in a high-pitched, goody-goody way. *Everyone says how brave I am! I always try my best!*

He sometimes had these thoughts himself about Elsa.

But over and over she proved that her goodness was internal. She never showed off. Her resoluteness was part of her, as if, very young, she'd made a decision to be good. Why? To protect her mother? With a survivor's instinct, he sensed that Margaret was breakable.

The house was hot and airless when Ida and Meyer returned from the Christmas party. Meyer put the sprinkler on his little front garden and they opened their bedroom window.

'What do you think of that nurse?' Ida said as they undressed.

'Which one?'

'You know! Sister Penny.'

'Strong, pleasant, very competent.'

'Attractive?'

He nodded his head from side to side. Meaning 'so so', 'not bad' or 'not my type'. He would never be brave enough, foolish enough, to answer *Yes! There is something rather special about her, she moves me in some way.* Even in the beginning, in that brief time before the war when they had been a glamorous young couple in Budapest, he was private, elusive. There would always be others. He would never talk about it. She would always be his wife.

He pulled back the curtain to let in the air.

'Are you tired?' he asked as they lay against their pillows in the moonlight.

'Exhausted. You?'

'Yes. But it was good today.'

'Good? Our son's first Christmas in a polio hospital?' Ida turned her head to look at him. This was the first time in months that she'd heard warmth in Meyer's voice.

'It was good,' he said again.

16.
The Verandah

After Christmas they were taken over by a heatwave so intense that it was like a time of war. It was all people talked about. Bushfires in the hills covered the city in a haze. There was a sense of emergency. Water restrictions were imposed. All inessential activity ceased.

Norm Whitehouse prowled around the garden in the blazing sun on a rescue mission with a watering can. The younger children no longer played on the little merry-go-round or in the paddling pool. It was school holidays, no day kids came, and some of the patients' families had left the city without them for holidays on the coast.

Lidja had gone for two weeks' sailing with her husband in Darwin. The nurses gave the children walking practice, but for this brief time even the daily business of rehabilitation did not seem as essential as staying cool. The Golden Age quietened and slowed, became its own self-contained world. The children lay in shorts and singlets on their beds, reading or drawing or playing games, while the old brass ceiling fans pushed hot air around. In Boys, Warren Barrett organised spit-ball competitions, until the boys lay sodden with spit and idiotic laughter and Sister Penny issued a ban. Each day seemed more oppressive than the one before. The babies wailed. The itchiness of sticky limbs inside the casts and splints could seem unbearable and the nurses took them in turn to cool down in the angel-bath.

After tea, at six o'clock, when the Netting Factory lights came on, they were allowed outside to sit on the verandah until they were tired enough to sleep. Above them on the balcony, the nurses lingered over their dinner. The clatter of their plates and their bursts of high-pitched laughter seeped into the summer dark. In the houses opposite, everyone had gone inside to eat.

Left on their own, like birds gathered at a waterhole at sundown, the children were revitalised, their thin voices echoing in the twilight. For once they felt as if they were the free spirits, rumbling up and down the broad timber boards of the verandah in the dusk. Warren Barrett and Malcolm Poole started off proceedings with a wheelchair scuffle, trying to crush each other's knuckles. Races were held, two in a heat, with handicaps for the bigger ones. Surprisingly, tiny Albert Sutton was a tearaway. At home, he told them shyly, they used to call him The Bolter.

Then a rowdy game of Keepings-Off was organised, with a beanbag instead of a ball, until the inevitable happened – somebody was hit, a wheelchair tipped, a howl issued from one of the little girls – and Ngaire or Hadley Dent, or Trixie Smith, the big new nurse who told them stories about growing up on a farm in the wheatbelt – arrived to settle everyone down.

Later in the evening they were watched by families in the houses across the road, sitting out on their porches after dinner, legs splayed, fanning themselves. Two boys and a big-boned girl played cricket barefoot on Alfred Street, their voices loud in the still air. Did they have to be so noisy? It was as if they were showing off how strong, how intact, they were. Sometimes they just hung around and stared.

Under these eyes, the Golden Age children once again saw themselves as a curiosity. Damaged creatures who could not move unaided. They recognised this for what it was: a preparation for their return to the world. But meanwhile, for once they were the ones having a good time. Warren Barrett even called out to a boy riding past who was eating hot chips and asked him to buy two bobs' worth for them. With everyone's odd sixpence or penny they managed to find the money, and the boy kept his word. The chips, numerically shared out, crunchy with hot fat and salt, were like a taste of life outside. After that they always kept a look-out for the boy on the bike, a mythical figure now, never again to materialise.

The sunset faded and the first star appeared. Like children everywhere on summer nights, they became free spirits, bold, vagabond, eerie, their grins reckless across their faces. The moon rose. The lights of the Netting Factory blinked on.

The verandah was a halfway existence, half-inside, half-out. It took them one step closer to normal life. They felt themselves lighten. This was their last stretch as patients. They were on their way back into the world.

*

Frank sat at the end of the verandah on his own, his prescription pad on his knee, a serious expression on his face. He chewed on his pencil and gazed into the distance, frowning a little as if in the throes of composition, the corner of his eye always on Elsa.

All the childhood years he had spent living side by side with strangers had taught him how to preserve himself. It was safer to watch, to plot your course, to judge your moment if there was something you really wanted.

Sitting next to Elsa was her favourite, Ann Lee, who was nine years old. Susan Bennett was eleven, closer in age to Elsa, but Susan was a goody-goody who sucked up to the nurses. Lucy Boyer and Julia Snow were six and seven, but they belonged only to themselves.

Frank wanted Elsa to himself, but who could be jealous of Ann Lee, so slight and pale she could almost melt into the twilight, so shy he hardly knew the sound of her voice, so grave he'd never seen her smile. She had black eyes and a sprinkle of unlikely freckles across her tiny nose. Her dead-straight black hair was cut by the nurses in the shape of a bowl. Beautiful hair, they said, her mother is Chinese. Keeping his eye on her as a rival, Frank came to understand that she, like him, watched and listened to everything around her.

Ann Lee came from Wiluna on the edge of the Gibson Desert, where her father worked in the mines. When he'd brought her to the Golden Age, hundreds of miles by truck and train, he'd carried her inside. She could only crawl and drag herself around.

For some weeks now, with callipers and mounted on tiny crutches, still unsmiling, she had been walking.

One evening a little white dog trotted past the verandah, its short legs going like beaters, its tongue hanging out. The children became as excited as if they'd seen a jungle beast. Whistling, clicking their fingers, their high voices mingled into a chorus: 'Here, boy!' With mugs of water they filled a bowl and left it as an offering at the edge of the verandah. But the dog raised its stumpy tail straight up like a flag and passed into the night.

Ann Lee's voice piped up, creaky as if from disuse. 'The horses will be thirsty.'

'What horses, Annie?' Elsa asked.

'The brumbies. When it hasn't rained they come to town looking for water. My mother always fills the trough for them.'

Her voice became high. It was because of the brumbies that she came to the Golden Age, she said. After she'd had polio, her parents brought her home from the Meekatharra hospital. She couldn't walk. One day her mother was called out to help a neighbour and had to leave her on her own for half an hour. Ann Lee was playing on the floor in the front room when she heard the sound of horses' hoofs and she crawled to the open door. A brumby stallion was leading a group of six horses to the trough in the front yard.

This year, her mother had been so busy with Ann Lee that she'd forgotten to fill the trough.

The stallion stood waiting, his head high, his nostrils twitching. Then he picked his way up the gravel path towards her and stood above her in the doorway. He bent down close to her, his gusts of hot breath all over her face. His eyes, huge, liquid, bulging, looked into hers. She knew what he

129

was asking. *Where is the water? We are dying of thirst. Why don't you help us?* She didn't know how long he stayed there. At last he backed away, turned, heels clipping down the path again. The other horses turned and followed him. Then in a pack they started running, out into the desert, the dust rising from their hoofs.

Ann Lee crawled away and hid behind the piano.

Right at that moment she decided that she would go with her father to the city so she could learn to walk. She must never ever be so helpless again. She must always be able to give a drink to thirsty creatures. The miners passed a hat around for their fares.

The Netting Factory lights came on, and the city glow rose and hung like powder in the darkening air. The nurses came bustling downstairs, and shepherded the children back inside. Frank stayed at the end of the verandah for as long as he could, his back turned, the prescription pad on his knee.

'You are the light that swirls around me,' he wrote.

'Darkness lies over the desert.'

17.

The Sea

It was decided that the Golden Age children needed a change of air. After the heatwave, they were quieter and paler and dangerously well behaved. It was important that they didn't lose heart. A day at the sea was prescribed.

Straight after breakfast all the patients and staff, except for Fabio, who had a temperature, and Sister Penny who stayed behind with him, were transported by Mrs Jewell the Red Cross volunteer in her ambulance to a bay down the coast, just past the outskirts of the suburbs. Here the sea was always calm and the little beach ran flat to the water. On weekdays it was deserted. Norm Whitehouse with Nella and the meals and a supply of towels followed Mrs Jewell in his ute. The rest of the nurses came in Trixie Smith's car. Everybody was in high spirits.

*

Across the road from the beach was an old weatherboard farmhouse with an iron roof, wide verandahs and a water tank. A great wind-twisted sheoak stood beside it. The place was owned by the Anglican Church, which hired it out for charitable ventures. Beside it a ridge of bush ran up the back of giant sandhills overlooking the ocean. Along the verandahs, protected from the wind by peppermint trees, were rows of ancient iron beds, each with a flabby kapok mattress and grey army blanket, where countless young Christians had slept. Here the Golden Age children could change in and out of swimsuits and store their crutches, callipers and braces. They could lie down if they were tired.

They were helped, carried, or piggy-backed by Norm and the nurses to the ocean's lapping edge.

The cure appeared to have immediate effect. The children sat on the shoreline in the ebb and flow of the waves, or were carried into the deeper water in the strong arms of a nurse. Everything was refreshing, the nurses in swimsuits showing their women's bodies, the sun freckling the children's pale faces, the cold swift water startling life into their poor limbs. They screamed and splashed and forgot their daily exertions on land.

Afterwards, they ate Nella's thick cheese or polony sandwiches with a glass of cold milk, their legs dangling off the edge of the verandah. They fooled and shouted, lighthearted, enjoying the sleek warmth across their shoulders, their mood expanding into the openness around them, their lungs recharged with fresh air. The sun shone on their thin limbs, their squinting eyes and bare white foreheads.

Only Elsa was quiet. This was *her* world, the ocean and its white sandhills and the streets behind, where once she'd lived and ridden her bike. She felt a clutch of loss, of posses-siveness. On the way here, Mrs Jewell had even driven down North Street, and through the back window of the ambu-lance she'd glimpsed her house, small and crouched, blinds pulled down for the heat as if it slept. Leaves drooped from the trees by the porch like dirty rags.

In the calm water she stood unsure and couldn't let go of Norm's arm. This was a shock. She who used to love the wild seas best, fighting the waves, picking herself up if she were dumped. Then riding home wet, downhill, without putting on the brakes.

The certain knowledge came to her during rest-time that whatever her achievements in the future, she would never again ride a bike around the river to Perth, or stand up to the dumpers on a windy day.

'Never' was a word you weren't allowed to say at the Golden Age. But now that she was walking, she often muttered it, to prepare herself for all she could no longer do.

Her bike was parked at the back of the garage at home, a Malvern Star, second-hand but spray-painted silver-blue, so much her steed that to her its headlamp was a nose, its handlebars antlers, its chainguard shaped like a wing. Malvern, her flying steed. The present for her tenth birthday. Sally would soon be ten. Did she ride Malvern now? Her parents mightn't say this, but would they think, *No need to buy a bike for Sally. There's Elsa's in the garage . . . she won't be needing it . . .*

Meanwhile Frank, on a bed on the verandah along the other side of the house, felt a poem coming on. He was lying down to be quiet. He knew as soon as he came into this old place that there was a poem here. Felt it as a squirm of excitement deep in his bowels. The bare wooden floors and walls, grey blankets, scrubby bush reminded him of the barracks where they had stayed when they first came to Australia. Just enough and no more. Just to let you know what you were worth. That's what his parents said. For weeks they'd smoked and smoked and had not smiled. He saw their disappointment, yet he felt only curiosity for everything around him, and the contentment he always felt when Meyer was with him. The poem had to incorporate all this. He was waiting for the first line.

The sea breeze started up and the peppermints rustled, their shadows dipping across the verandah. Once there was a lake as big as a sea, with beaches, wooden summer houses, pine forests. Frank had no memory of it. Yet he carried the word 'Balaton' with him like a shadow existence.

Everything then happened in another language. He only knew a few words now. Ida and Meyer used Hungarian for secrets between them, and with Hungarian friends. They wanted Frank to grow up speaking English.

English excited him, he wanted to take possession of it. To express all that had been lost.

This poem was the link between the two worlds – water, trees, wooden walls . . . but the light here was different . . . how to convey the *atmosphere* of each . . .

He fell asleep.

After the siesta and an afternoon paddle, the children were dressed and braced and kitted up again. Nella, her face and arms red from the sun, heated up a vat of pea soup on the woodstove in the kitchen and the children ate, for once with appetite, sitting along the edge of the front verandah. They were instructed to watch the sun sink below the horizon and see if they could catch sight of the rare green flash that sometimes occurred in the moment of its disappearance. Nella said it meant you'd get your heart's desire. They could hear the nurses laughing as they washed the dishes. Everyone was in a good mood. Frank, avid for luck, didn't take his eyes off the horizon. Then all the children shouted, claiming to have seen the green flash. Perhaps they'd all made the same wish – to be a normal child again.

Their cure was thorough, a whole day's worth. Now, at twilight, the water turned milky green, the mauve sky shaded into grey. They were waiting to spot the evening star rise up over the horizon. A liner was passing, they could see the lights on the deck and two little funnels. Perhaps it was the Queen of England sailing past on her way to Sydney with the Duke on the Royal Yacht, the *Gothic*! They waved and cheered.

When Frank looked around again, Elsa had disappeared.

All day he'd felt close to her. He knew this was her world. Her eyes were blue as the water, her hair as pale as the sand. But Elsa had been quiet.

A lone seagull circled, crying, and he knew that she was sad. He picked up his crutches and made his way around the corner to the side verandah where he'd slept that afternoon. She was leaning against the rail, slumped a little, chin in hand, crutches next to her. Waiting for him. The grey-green bush in the gully glowed luminous for a few moments. The air was filled with the mad twitter of little birds. And there it was, the evening star twinkling high above the dark mass of the sandhills.

Just when I thought
I'd never find you
You appear.

Why did these word arrangements only occur when he saw Elsa? Love was instantaneous, like inspiration. He touched the prescription pad in his pocket. He was still unable to finish 'On My Last Day on Earth'. Most of the poems he wrote now were for Elsa. They could be called 'On My First Day on Earth'.

He stood close beside her. A coolness radiated from her skin after the water. She was looking out across the bush, alive with the frantic bedtime chatter of its creatures.

'I wish we could sleep here,' she said.

'So do I.'

'In the open air. Like animals.'

'If we were animals, you'd be one of those pale gold horses with a white mane.'

'A Palomino. What would you be?'

'A fox, following a Palomino.'

She stared at him for a moment, then broke into a laugh.

Frank didn't laugh. It was true. He would have liked to sniff his nose up and down her gleaming skin.

'"We walk with four legs now",' he said, waving his two crutches.

It was a line he'd been working on.

She laughed again. This funny boy – sharp, watchful, personal, not like a boy really, or any boy she'd ever known. Right from the start Frank had acted as if they were members of a secret club. A two-member club to which she'd just been elected. He was shorter than her and, she suspected, less robust. They were both born in 1941 – Frank in January, she in July. Last week his parents had brought a birthday cake to the Golden Age for everyone to share. Frank was now thirteen. They knew about each other's parents, teachers, the friends they used to have. Everything they liked or hated, food, books, film stars, wireless programmes. The smell of their skin and breath. The taste of their mouths. Sometimes, away from other people, a gap opened up that was almost like pain, and without words they drew together across it like magnets and kissed. They had to. Her heart thumped now whenever she saw him.

There was something hungry about him. She knew, she'd watched him. His first thought always was to grab what he wanted. He didn't try to hide it. He ate the jam first in the roly-poly and when he thought no one was looking, reached for another piece. He ate the icing on the Jubilee Twist, and the thick cold butter on the scones. He knew what he liked and he took it. Was this because he was caught in the war when he was a little kid?

He was always writing words down in his old prescription pad. He said they were poems, but they didn't rhyme. Could poetry be like that? She half-suspected that his poetry writing was a pose.

She didn't know how much she liked him. Whenever she tried to think about this, her mind slid away. She sat next to him quietly, her hands folded like a woman.

But she missed him when he left a room. Everything was suddenly boring. A light went out. Every morning when she woke, she listened for the sound of his voice. Usually she could hear it somewhere in the building. He was a talker. He often spoke about whether he was or was not friends with someone. This was important to him. He was always on and off with one of the staff – Hadley, Nella, Mrs Simmons. Elsa was the best friend he'd ever had, he said.

She knew that whenever she left a room, or disappeared around a corner of the verandah, he would come looking for her.

Alone, she sometimes practised the little twist of his vowels, the occasional use of 'v' for 'w', like a New Australian.

Something had happened to her in these past few days. If she didn't see him she missed him. He *haunts* me, she thought.

The nurses were calling them.

'Want to hear the next line?' he said, as they set off.

'All right.'

' "Slowly we are turning into something else".'

'You mean – teenagers?'

He shook his head.

'What else?'

'I'll tell you when I know.'

The backs of their hands brushed as they walked side by side on their crutches. Their bloodstreams recharged by exercise and fresh air, they experienced a fiery burst of pleasure.

18.

A Long Cool Drink

The front door of the Golden Age was always open, from six in the morning when Norm Whitehouse brought in the milk bottles, until nine, or even later at night if some of the nurses went out. Who would ever dream of stealing from a children's polio hospital? Besides, Sister Penny didn't want the door shut to any parent who might suddenly have a chance or need to see their child, nor to the life and sounds of the outside world. In the entrance hall there were two long seats where you could wait if everyone was busy.

Mid-afternoon Sister Penny came into the hallway to see Meyer Gold standing there, a wooden crate of bottles at his feet.

'Mr Gold! All the children are at the beach today!'

'I forgot!' Meyer slapped his palm against his forehead.

'I was driving up Thomas Street and I thought *vot da hell*, I'll give the kids a treat.'

'Fabio's here, but he's sick . . . It's just Fabio and me, I'm afraid.'

Behind him, parked on Alfred Street, she saw a green truck with 'Bickford's Cool Drinks' in yellow letters on the cab door.

'That's very kind of Bickford's . . .'

'Bickford's can go to hell! This is *my* gift.'

'Just the thing to pick them up when they get back.' Her smile was wide, gracious, a benefactor's due.

She led the way to the kitchen. The quiet was strange. Light flowed unhindered down the polished linoleum runner along the corridor. Open doors yielded glimpses of empty beds, white space and order.

He put the crate down by Nella's fridge and, crouching at the open door, started to poke bottles of Bickford's Ginger Beer, neck first, into spare corners of the intricately packed interior.

'Take care, Mr Gold!' For some reason his actions made Sister Penny want to laugh. 'For Nella this fridge is a *person*.'

Meyer kept out one bottle. He found iceblocks in the narrow freezer tray, and two glasses. As he poured, the glasses erupted into a fizz of pale brown bubbles. 'This is really quite refreshing in the heat,' he said. 'Cheers!'

She laughed, liking to hear the local words in his accent. 'Cheers!' she said. They clinked glasses, suddenly light-hearted.

They sat at the table. He told her how he had changed jobs. The brother of a fellow worker at the bike factory was starting up a cool drink business and needed a driver. 'I told him I was a driver. Then in my lunchbreak I rushed to take my test. Thanks God I pass! In Hungary I used to drive all the time. I love to drive. But, to be honest, I never have worked as a driver in my life.'

'What did you do in Hungary?'

'Ran the family business. Imports and exports.'

'Do you like this job?'

'It's my ideal, I think! I'm alone, outside, free to move and look around. I'm beginning to understand this city.'

'Understand what?'

'That it is its own place. It is not like anywhere else.'

An *incongruously* beautiful woman, he was thinking, looking at her wide, smooth, burnished cheeks, her full, composed mouth. Why incongruous? Why be surprised by beauty in this country? There was beauty everywhere, strange beauty, even – especially? – in a children's polio hospital. Was this what was making him happy? It had always been here but he hadn't seen it. As if the old world had finally taken its hands from his eyes.

A *natural*. When he looked at her, that was the word that came to him. Everything about her was generous. A wave of thick, honey-coloured hair was rolled back from her forehead. Her body was sturdy, rounded, dedicated to action. Her health gave off warmth, like an advertisement for her profession.

There was a light inside her.

Odd people kept coming back to him. Ones he didn't know he missed. As if he were visited. For the past few weeks he'd been seeing, or dreaming of, his brother Janos's Protestant girlfriend, Suszi: her calm ways, her mannish pants and shirts, the little cough as her lungs weakened. A heroine. She'd helped them all.

The good people were extraordinary.

He could feel a look coming over his face as he met this nurse's eyes, a look that he'd forgotten, like a silky mask slipping over his head, smoothing his wrinkles, outlining his jaw. A mask through which his eyes watched, keen as a hunter's, with a gambler's glint of irony. A little smile hovered on his lips.

Everything seemed like an echo from the unrecoverable past.

'I must go,' he said, putting down his glass.

Watch the parents as much as the child, she told her nurses. The Golds were quiet people. There was something chilly and measured, fragile, about their joys. Sadness had sharpened Ida's face. Looking into Meyer Gold's eyes now, she sensed for a moment the dense life inside him, all he'd loved and given up.

'Would you like a sandwich?'

'Thanks. I have eaten.'

'A cup of tea?'

Meyer noted and dismissed an impulse to pull her into his lap. His legs tingled, a long-lost sensation. He watched her find the matches, light the gas, put on the kettle. Not quite as decisive and quick as she was in the wards. Was this a woman who had given up domesticity?

'Do you have a kitchen of your own somewhere?'

'No. I live here.'

'Where do you go to be alone?'

'To the beach.' She smiled, pleased that he recognised this need.

'Do you swim in the ocean?'

'When it warms up. Sometimes far out. There comes a point where I have to make myself turn back. I walk for miles along the sand. I sleep in the sun. I try to get as far away from other people as possible.'

He suddenly remembered the vision a couple of weeks ago, the hollow sound of the train rushing into Leederville station like a wave crashing onto the edge of the ocean. The words it brought: *Lie down with me*.

A droning noise had started up in the nursery.

'Believe it or not, that's Fabio singing. He must be feeling better.' She smiled at Meyer from the doorway. 'Thanks for the drink.'

As he walked past the nursery, the droning stopped and he heard her clear laughter, like sunlight.

Out in the heat again, in the cab of the truck, he watched the high brick chimneys of the Golden Age recede in the rear-vision mirror. Under any one roof, at any one time, he thought, there is always a couple of creatures a little in love with one another.

Once you have tasted meaninglessness, you lose any idea of reward, or punishment, or conventional virtue.

He only knew that he couldn't afford to lose one more thing.

The heat and brightness hit him straight in the eyes when he entered the northern highway. He'd have to buy sunglasses. But the roads here, the long steady run of them, the space and flatness soothed him. They suited the thinness of his spirit.

To the north, the houses dwindled, huddled, roofs poking up out of the glare of the sandhills.

I wonder if there's a poet growing up here somewhere, Meyer thought.

19.

Lidja

The date passed for Lidja's return from the holiday with her husband in Darwin. A week went by. It was most unlike Lidja, who was so precise, so committed to the children's progress.

One evening when all the children were together on the verandah, Sister Penny came out of the office and told them that she had just received a phone call from Lidja's sister. There had been a sailing accident. The yacht which Lidja and her husband had been sailing had sunk and Lidja had disappeared without a trace. She was presumed drowned.

Sister Penny was not a believer, and could not go on to say that Lidja had gone to heaven. Some of the nurses thought they should have said a little prayer. Some thought that the children should not have been told at all. But Sister Penny had an aversion to secrets and whispers, and believed it was best for the children to hear the truth at once, when they were all together. Hadley and Ngaire, red-eyed, brought out glasses of warm milk. They took the younger children inside to prepare for bed. Frank and Elsa stayed out a few minutes longer in the soft warm air. Then they could walk together on their crutches unhindered by the others in the corridor. There was comfort in the touch of their shoulders, the brushing of their hands.

As they were cleaning their teeth, side by side in adjacent basins, Frank asked Elsa if she thought a shark would have eaten Lidja. Elsa rinsed and spat, met his eyes and nodded, yes.

A temporary physiotherapist called Moira, newly arrived from Scotland, came to work with them. She had auburn hair, dazzling, translucent skin, a brisk but good-tempered manner and lilting accent – 'Och, you're a bonny wee bairn!' – that the children didn't always understand. It took them a while to respond to the Scottish physiotherapist, as she was called at first, because they missed Lidja, her great sad black eyes, her worries over them, her lectures on persistence, or what she called 'character'. They could still hear her voice as they practised. '*Think* those muscles in your foot! *Make* them come back.'

They longed for her, like a mother.

Over and over, it seemed, they were reminded that they were alone, that in the end, their success or failure in overcoming polio was up to them.

20.

The Queen

For a week or two it looked as though the royal visit in March would not take place because of polio. This possibility made headlines, day after day. Since January, ninety-six cases had been reported in Perth. A marching display in Her Majesty's honour by 30,000 schoolkids at the Showgrounds was cancelled. Nobody talked of anything else. At the Golden Age the children felt a sort of guilt, even though they were all long out of quarantine.

In the end it was decided that the visit would go ahead, but as if there were an invisible wall between the people of Perth and the royal couple. The Queen and Duke would sleep and eat on the *Gothic*, berthed in Fremantle. No gifts or bouquets would be accepted personally by Her Majesty, no shaking of hands. A certain distance would at all times be maintained.

The local Rotary Club took everyone from the Golden Age, including Norm, Nella and the Scottish physiotherapist, in a hired bus one twilight to see their modest, reserved little city transformed into streets of colossal celebration. Huge illuminated arches topped with glittering crowns reached across St Georges Terrace. Giant portraits of the royal couple surrounded by Union Jacks were draped across building fronts; banners were hung from every window on the city block proclaiming 'God Save the Queen'.

Each time the children came into the Golden Age hallway they stopped to gaze at the large, coloured photograph of the young Queen and the Duke, gilt-framed, hanging just above their heads. Her face had become familiar to them, she was everywhere, like a beautiful godmother, angel or film star, girlishly pretty with her round cheeks, curly hair and wide, lovely smile, her softness and goodness protected by her upright, hard-faced soldier prince. 'Our Lady' little Albert Sutton called her. Even the busy nurses paused in front of the portrait.

'Do you think he's crazy about her?' Frank heard Ngaire say. 'Or was it all arranged?'

Suddenly everybody felt the urge to do their best, as if they were each about to undergo a personal royal inspection. Lewis gave up sucking his thumb. Fabio stopped wetting the bed. Frank walked everywhere now with a stick. Elsa, in callipers, walked with crutches or holding hands with Ann Lee. Some days she had to return to using her chair because she had overdone it.

In spite of the water restrictions Norm's lawn was nursed into greenness, and his roses, pink and scented, under the shelter of an umbrella, were in perfect bloom. It was as if the whole city were waiting for the royal stamp of approval.

Only the Golds seemed immune to the excitement.

What monarchists they are, Meyer thought, these colonials. A tiny lost tribe on the coast of a huge island, faithfully waiting for a ship from the Motherland.

Didn't they understand what had happened to the old countries of Europe?

Susan Bennett was keeping a scrapbook of The Visit. The staff gave her newspapers and magazines. Her parents, Tikka and Rodney, had been invited to the Royal Garden Party at Government House. Susan said this was because her father was a public servant. The phrase intrigued Frank. Did Mr Bennett hire himself out to the public as a cleaner, a gardener, a sweeper of the streets?

One evening Frank caught sight of Rodney Bennett when he and Tikka dropped into the Golden Age, which was rare. A grown-up man with a boy's face, round rosy cheeks, yellow wavy hair, a maroon striped blazer, white shoes and white pants. Tikka smiled and smiled, showing all her teeth. She left a trail of scent behind her that the children in the room could smell all night. Susan was not as good-looking as her parents.

Elsa suddenly remembered that Susan's swimsuit was even older and more perished than hers, so loose she was embarrassed.

Visitors often forgot that the curtains around each bed blocked sight, not sound. Behind Susan's curtains Tikka and Rodney were loud. They had come from something they called 'cocktails', they sounded excited. Elsa heard everything they said. They were talking about who had or hadn't been invited to the garden party. 'We thought that, you know, with *you* being *here*, we'd be crossed off the list,' Tikka said to Susan.

They left, waving at everyone, like famous people, promising to call in straight after the garden party to tell Susan all about it, blowing her kisses.

On the afternoon of the garden party, Susan, in bed, was unable to read or sleep. She recited the details of her mother's outfit to anyone who would listen: *eau de nil* voile, cream suede bag and shoes, a toque of emerald feathers. She completed that day's clipping and pasting into her scrapbook and lay quite still with her eyes open, long after lights out. She was still awake at ten that night when Trixie Smith did her rounds.

'I wouldn't wait up any longer if I were you,' Trixie said grimly. Susan was feverish, her eyes glittery. Trixie gave her half an aspirin and slipped her a chocolate.

But the next day she was up again, working even harder than usual, *helping*, wheeling the babies, reading them stories, sharpening pencils for the younger children.

The Bennetts called in during the week. They were full of chatter, still excited. The Queen's magnificent complexion. The Government House gardens. The couple they had met in the queue. They'd made new friends!

Elsa heard Susan's voice like a little child's: 'Why didn't you come?'

The Bennetts knew instantly what she meant.

'Snoggins, it was *impossible*! You should have seen the traffic!'

'Sit up, darling. I'm going to comb your hair.'

Rodney was thirsty and went to the kitchen. He came back shaking his head. 'That Nella! What a character! I asked her for a glass of water and she pointed to the sink and turned her back!'

The Golden Age children were delivered by Mrs Jewell in the ambulance to the roadside outside Princess Margaret Hospital, where they joined the hospital patients already lined up in chairs, some even on stretchers. Was there a tiny hope that at this touching sight the Queen would order the chauffeur to stop and descend like an angel to bless them? Or at least offer them some special acknowledgement?

The excitement when the black Daimler appeared behind its escort of police on motorcycles was almost suffocating. As the car rolled past, the children sighted an arm in a long white glove, waving back and forward like something mechanical. A glimpse of that youthful smile, gleaming teeth in the shadows, the stern outline of the Duke's profile. All the children called out 'Hooray! Hooray!', even Frank, who had no ancestral feeling for Her Majesty at all. Julia Snow and Lucy Boyer clutched each other. Susan Bennett turned pale and thought she was going to be sick.

Ida didn't visit Frank at this time because she was spending every spare moment after work practising for the Queen's Concert. Also having fittings for a new dress made by her friend Dora Fink, who had worked for a couturier in Vienna.

Meyer said that it made him happy to wake up to the sound of scales being played every morning.

'She is very nervous, Feri. Her last performance was in the camp in Vienna. Do you remember that concert? The soprano, the choir, the magician.'

'I remember the magician.'

'That was in forty-seven. After that she didn't touch a piano for years.'

In his new job with Bickford's, Meyer often dropped in to see Frank. He sank down, relaxed, beside Frank on the verandah, or sat on Frank's bed – brief visits, his eyes taking in everything around him. Just letting the engine cool down, he said. Because of the heat, he wore shorts and workboots and a white shirt with the sleeves rolled up. On the whitest, brightest days he wore a cheap straw hat turned up at the sides, like a cowboy. He was tanned dark brown. No one would ever think that he was pale Frank's father. Or that he had once been a sophisticate, a businessman. There were white lines creasing the corners of his eyes.

Frank said, 'You smile more.'

'Do I?' Meyer was rolling himself a cigarette. 'I like to be outside. As a boy in Balaton all my life was lived in the open air.' He put the cigarette in his pocket. It was the end of the day, he was on his way home.

'You look different,' Frank said.

'You know what, Feri? The past seems further away.'

It was an admission that Meyer hadn't even thought about till then. It took him by surprise. Yet as he spoke, from one second to the next, he realised that everything had changed. What had been temporary had become settled. What had seemed like the end of the world had become the centre. He was beginning to understand that this experience was not inferior, but had its own nature, its own mysterious significance. *It was all that he needed.* Meyer's hand went into

152

his pocket and came out again. Frank knew all his moves. Whenever he had a thought he wanted to smoke.

Frank watched Meyer as he strode down the verandah and leapt off without using the steps. He always lit up as he left. High above, banking clouds had turned the light greenish. The dogs barked all the way down Alfred Street as the Bickford's truck rattled past.

A 'floral presentation', one of the many bouquets that had been placed, untouched, onto a table for Her Majesty to inspect, was delivered to the Golden Age on the day that she left. Everybody took photos of it, or cut pieces of the ribbon as mementos. Flowers that the Queen had looked at!

Sister Penny wrote to thank her on behalf of the children, and a month later received a letter back from the Queen's lady-in-waiting, Lady Pamela Mountbatten. It too became a holy relic, mounted behind glass, hanging in the hall beside the Queen's portrait.

The Queen survived Western Australia uninfected, and the visit was pronounced to have been a tremendous success.

A week or two after the *Gothic* had sailed off across the Indian Ocean, however, half a dozen new cases of polio were reported, contracted amongst the crowds gathered by the roadsides to see her.

At the same time, the March 1954 edition of *Time Magazine* featured on its cover a portrait of the handsome young Jewish doctor Jonas Salk, and below him were the words 'Is this the year?' A year later the announcement would flash around the world that it had indeed been the year that his polio vaccination had proved to be successful. The children's summer plague would soon be something that happened in the past.

21.
Ida and Meyer

On the day of the concert, late afternoon, Meyer as usual parked the truck at Bickford's yard in Newcastle Street and rode Frank's bike back home. For the past week now he'd arrived to the sound of the piano. Ida had worked half-days at the milliner's so she could use the afternoons to practise. She was playing the Mozart piece again when he let himself in, a good choice, he thought. Would hook everyone in, even the little ones, or those who didn't know anything about classical music, which, he supposed, might be most of the audience.

He stood in the front hall, sweaty, dirty, a working man, transfixed for a moment by the perfect notes, felt almost as a pain in his body, swirling like dust in the low rays of the sun.

She was playing more convincingly. After weeks of practice, something else had entered. What? It gave him the old feeling of excitement. He'd felt it the first moment he'd ever heard her. A lightness, a pace of her own that became a voice. Others had heard it too, he knew at once from the quality of their silence. In Budapest, in Vienna, in all of Europe she would have become celebrated. Who knows to what degree? And to what degree did she still have that power? So much time lost. She insisted it was over. Wouldn't even entertain his speculations about starting up again here. This was no place for a serious musician, she said. Her career was in the past, like Europe.

He sometimes thought she enjoyed saying this. It was easier than practising. It was her revenge on Fate. Her revenge on him. For what? The disappointments of their life? Her listlessness discouraged him. He'd been meaning to talk about it with her, and then Frank had got sick. Then there *was* an urgency, a point to everything they did, a deal to make. Though not with God.

God did not exist.

Tonight's performance was a thank-you note for Frank's recovery. To the Golden Age, but also to Fate. They could not risk ingratitude. He knew the way Ida thought. Like many artists she was superstitious. Perhaps it was a way of coping with the capriciousness of talent. The infinite pains it took. She made it known that this was it, the final performance. Never again. She'd said this before, when Frank was in Intensive Care. That time she was making a bargain. Her art for Frank's survival.

She turned her head to him when he came into the room. Her face looked dry and hot. Her eyes were sunken and her hair pulled into a lopsided knot, all the grey showing. The blinds were pulled down, there was no air moving.

She was wearing only her slip and her shoulders looked thin and white.

'Don't stop.'

'If they heard me play like this at home, they would throw me out. The mistakes! I am months away from being ready for this, Meyer. I really cannot play. It will be a parody of a concert, a travesty, a joke.'

Home. She hadn't called Hungary that for years. She was talking of somewhere else. Her place in music.

'Ida, this audience will not be judging you. The children are very excited.'

'How do you know?'

'I called in with the truck on my way back.'

'You are there all the time now,' she said sourly. 'Ferenc sees much more of you than of me.'

'Idona, go and run a bath. Then we will eat.'

'I have to practise. Even for these people.' Her pointy face could easily express snobbery: mouth and nostrils pulled tight, eyes cold and haughty.

'All people respond to excellence, even if they don't know what it is they are hearing.'

'That is why it is *unforgivable* to perform if you are out of practice. A *sin*.' She turned back to the keys. He loved, most of all, her strong, clever fingers, plain, pale, workmanlike, greasy-looking, the nails clipped short. The work they did for her. The mind, the hands that made the music were the best part of her, the most moral, the most generous.

Suddenly the buzz and lightness in his head lifted: he was standing in a small, stuffy room, listening to a summation of all the tragedy and beauty of his life.

She always did it, just for a moment, gave him back to himself.

He went and stood behind her, put his hands on her shoulders. He bent down and whispered in her ear, 'You are going to give them something lovely.'

She jerked away from him.

'I've just remembered! They've asked me to start with their awful anthem.' Her hands began to block out the chords of 'God Save the Queen'.

'*Our* anthem,' Meyer said, as he left to light the chip heater for her bath. For a moment the roar of its tiny fire reminded him of the wind on a beach. The hollow sound of the ocean . . . Where were they coming from, these visions? Sky, sea, the beach? Like a recurring dream. The word came to him: 'home'. He put his hand under the tap. The water was just past blood temperature. In the last rays of the sun, the purple oleander blossoms outside the bathroom louvres turned a deep glowing red.

After a performance, he remembered, Ida liked to sit down and accept a glass of brandy. She was simple, at peace, grateful with relief. Her skin went very soft.

He shouted down the hall for her to come and have a bath. Now, or they would miss the tram. He realised that he was enjoying this flurry, this turmoil. When Ida was performing, something came alive between them.

22.

The Concert

There was no doubt that they had done their best. Ida closed her eyes when she saw it, took a breath. She was standing at the window of the Golden Age kitchen, looking into the quadrangle, a concrete paved area bounded on three sides by the kitchen, the Covered Way and the New Treatment Block. Norm Whitehouse and some fathers had wheeled the piano from the schoolroom down the wheelchair ramps, into the centre of the quadrangle. Trixie Smith's fiancé, an electrician, had set up a spotlight on the fire escape outside the Nurses Quarters, and was still adjusting its direction onto the piano. Hired fold-up chairs were set out in rows on the lawn, all the way back to the straggling hibiscuses against the wire fence. A programme, cyclostiled, was laid on every seat. It included the request not to clap *at all* until the end of the three pieces. Ida was only too aware of the pitfalls of playing for the inexperienced concertgoer.

At least the wind had dropped. Out here, the Netting Factory throb was only just discernible . . . the music would block it out. Ida turned the kitchen light off, and watched the night softly seeping into the courtyard. Suddenly she saw herself in her black dress, at the window, alone, watching her audience trickle in. It was eternal, this moment, this solitude, no matter where you were performing or for whom.

She felt alert to everything that could happen. Her greatest fear came back to her. Humiliation.

In the meeting held to discuss the concert, some parents had suggested other items as well – recitations by the children, songs in a choir. Somebody mentioned that Albert Sutton's father told jokes semi-professionally at pubs or Trades Hall dinners. Ida, chin lifted, looked steadily out of the window while this was discussed. It was decided to keep the evening as a solo piano recital.

She wanted to give them something, something they would remember. She wanted the children to know what the piano could do. Now, too late, she saw her hubris.

Nurses were bringing in the children, the little ones in their dressing gowns, seating them in the front row, the smallest near the exit. They were chattering like little parrots at sundown, very excited, looking over their shoulders to spot their families or anyone they might know.

The teacher whom Frank called Mrs Cinnamon arrived with a well-built older girl who could only be her daughter, and Mrs Jewell, the ambulance driver, was sitting next to a white-haired man, Mr Jewell, she supposed.

There was Roy from the Princess Margaret splint shop, and Nella's husband, short and round as her – together they were a pair of Russian dolls. And some of the young men who came from the Apex Club to play board games with

160

the children, in white shirts and ties, fresh-shaven, with big, clean ears, ushering their fiancées into seats.

The night was warm and still, a party-like excitement in the air.

On a trestle table near the exit ramp, Meyer had set out hired glasses.

Bickford's had donated five crates of cool drinks. Meyer was keeping extra bottles cool in the New Treatment Wing, with a sack of ice emptied into the angel bath. Women set down plates covered with tea towels at one end of the trestle table. The audience, young and old, laughed and chatted, exuberant in the novelty of the occasion and the soft summer night.

Two policemen came on their night rounds, took off their hats and sat down in the front row, their large legs crossed. These seats were reserved for the older children, but no one liked to ask them to leave. Sister Penny ignored them as she welcomed other guests. After a few minutes, to the nurses' relief, the policemen, self-conscious, stood up and, placing their hats back on, sauntered towards the exit, where they lingered at the refreshment table.

It was quite likely that none of these people, except for Meyer and probably Frank, if he'd admit it, were listeners who could judge, or truly appreciate her performance, yet she must do her very best.

She was dying for a cigarette. How she rustled! The dress – sleeveless, close-fitting, a swathe of blue-black taffeta – crackled every time she moved. It could have held its own in New York or Paris. Dora Fink was ecstatic.

What could she have been thinking? She had somehow imposed Budapest Concert Hall onto this hospital courtyard!

An *émigrée artiste* nostalgic for her former fame . . . Revealing her vanity, her yearning to impress!

She had never felt so foreign, so absurdly out of place. She hoped that in this darkening twilight she was no more visible in the kitchen window than a shadow.

It was just past seven. The stars were coming out. The hired chairs were suddenly occupied. All the older children were now seated in the front row, wheelchairs and crutches neatly lined up by the exit ramp.

Frank was sitting in the middle of the front row, next to Elsa, the blonde girl who was his age. The stage light caught on her burnished temples, the golden wave of her hair. Frank needed a haircut. His abundant dark red curls were quite bouffant over his high forehead. He was animated, joking about something. Every cell in his body, she saw, was alert to the female next to him, his fate now in her hands.

Where was Meyer? There he was, she could just make out the shape of his body, standing, legs crossed, arms folded, in the shadows along the wall of the Treatment Block. On guard. For a stray gust of wind, a sudden summer shower, a drunk, a howling child. Everything went smoothly when Meyer was around. Nothing escaped him. Meyer was always in charge.

How remote he is, Sister Penny thought. He sees everything from a distance. She was standing at the top of the ramp, waiting to go on stage. It didn't look as if Elizabeth Ann was going to make it after all. Of course she was currently on teaching practice in a large kindergarten in Maylands and was *exhausted*, but she'd said on the phone she would try to come. She'd also mentioned that Tim – Tim Budd – hated classical music.

Most of the seats were occupied now. Frank's white face, Elsa's streams of pale hair became translucent in the creeping dark. The policemen had sunk into spare seats in the back row, and once again removed their hats.

Sister Penny stood under the spotlight making a speech. Pronouncing Boo-da-pest like a flyspray, steadily ploughing through all the foreign names of Ida's prizes. As if they meant anything to these people. The light outlined her sturdy height, her broad shoulders and the halo of fine golden hairs waving free around her head. Ida stood ready on the kitchen steps.

How lucky they were in Australia, Sister Penny was saying, to receive such talent on their shores. Ida had never heard that said before.

'We are truly honoured.' Sister Penny turned, raising her arm to welcome Ida. It was as if she held a light. Yes, she thought, as she smiled at Ida, the Golds had brought something new into her life, though she couldn't name it. Their sharp attentiveness, like witnesses, and the different way they saw things . . . their expectation of relating closely to you . . . their frankness . . .

Someone started clapping, others followed. Ida rustled out to her seat at the piano. 'Wind me up,' she muttered to herself in Hungarian, as she had from her very first performance, 'and off I go.' She had to say it every time. Mysteriously, it never failed her.

After 'God Save the Queen', executed as rapidly as possible, while the able-bodied in the audience half-rose and quickly subsided, she paused for a moment, rubbing her hands together. Then, taking a breath, bowing her head low over the keyboard, her hands suddenly dived, like a surgeon's into the cavity of a chest, Sister Penny thought.

'*A vous dirai-je*' – a clear voice in greeting to the children, its pure notes a salute to childhood, and, as it gathered momentum, a promise for the richness of childhood's future, for the joy of all the summer nights to come.

The policemen stayed for the entire piece. Then for the next, Schumann's 'Scenes from Childhood', and the next, Schubert's 'Impromptus'.

Mozart, Schumann, Schubert.

Nobody had ever heard anything like it.

She played very fast, bare-armed like a workman, with the conviction of one who must finish a job. The dress enthralled them, its blue-black shining folds, and Ida's strong white arms, her black hair in a roll, her faintly slanted Hungarian eyes were inexpressibly exotic. They knew that wherever she came from, she must have been famous there.

The children sat very still, some with their mouths open, or slowly chewing a finger. Some were grave, others looked almost triumphant, as if at last an expectation had been fulfilled. They didn't take their eyes off Ida's hands and her serious, distant face. The music filled the courtyard at once, like a rain squall, like walking into the light and noise of the Royal Show. Even the little ones did not move. A good proportion of their lives had been spent in the hushed white world of a hospital.

Malcolm Poole felt a satisfaction, as if numbers were falling into place, something right clicking in his brain. A shiver of relaxation ran through his slight, twisted body.

Tears ran down Ngaire's face. Her mother had taught piano in Auckland, but Ngaire, her mother said, didn't have a musical bone in her body. They often quarrelled. Ngaire, very young, had run away with a man to Sydney and soon after that her mother died. One night the man didn't come home. Ngaire read a recruitment advertisement for nurses in Western Australia and spent the last of her savings on a ticket on the Trans-Australian Express.

Everything she did now, Ngaire thought, was for her mother, to prove she'd turned out all right.

Lastly Ida played Bach, 'Sheep May Safely Graze', a candle lit for the children's bedtime.

It was over. She had made three mistakes. Very small ones.

The clapping started slowly, out of dead silence, and then was fierce and cumulative. Nobody spoke. Ida recognised its sincerity, shivered, stood up, bowed.

Others started standing, then everybody except the children stood. 'Bravo!' someone called out. 'World class!' shouted Rodney Bennett. She would have played an encore except she knew that the children would be tired. When she'd finished playing, and let her hands fall in her lap, she'd turned her head and seen the row of small, white, serious faces. They'd listened to every note.

Bowing her head quickly in all directions, her eyes caught Frank's and she gave him one of her rare, ironic smiles. For a moment all was forgiven between them – how he'd regularly stolen from her purse, what a snob she'd been to his friends – all was understood. Watching her play, Frank was moved. He saw her strength, her vast determination.

He remembered her fury when he was in hospital. 'You are going to get strong! You are going to walk!'

'Mama, please!'

'You want to know why? They take the weak ones first.'

Everything was always about the war.

Now, behind the audience, outlined by streetlights, Ida saw the silhouette of neighbours who had crossed the road and stood listening at the fence. They too were applauding. Ida looked up. The moon had risen, full and yellow over the roofs of the local houses. She bowed again. It was all worth it, every time, for the thankfulness she felt, the peace, at the end of a concert. No matter who the audience.

Elsa, as senior girl, without stick or crutches made the short distance to Ida at the piano and presented her with a bouquet of Norm's roses. *How she has come on!* Jack thought. The music had opened him up in some way, returned him to himself. He found himself wishing that Margaret could have seen Elsa do this. That just for once Nance could have offered to mind Jane. He'd brought Sally, in Nance's car. With Nance.

Sister Penny invited everybody to supper and cool drinks. Meyer saw her from a distance tonight. As always, out of uniform she looked larger, more matronly, official. Any connection between them seemed hallucinatory, like the sound of the ocean if you held a shell to your ear. Ida's music took him back to his own country, his old self.

In the audience he'd seen the Sutton family file in, one daughter, five brothers. He'd had to take a breath. He could name the hierarchy as they sat down, one after the other. The eldest, the second son, the daughter . . . the third son was the gentle boy. Janos. He shuddered. A chill climate could be opened up like a window.

He remembered his dream from last week. He was in the camp, in the Carpathian Mountains. Rain, rain, he was saying, holding his tongue out. As if he was suffering from a terrible thirst.

Where was his son now? Meyer kept his eye on Frank as much as possible. Illness could make you prey to melancholy. There was a history of it in the Gold family. He saw that Frank and Elsa had left their seats and were standing at the side of the ramp. They looked serious, detached from everybody else. The light from the doorway shimmered around them. Meyer felt a pang – was it for his own youth? He who no longer fell in love.

After he'd taken Ida home, he would go for a walk. Walk for miles and miles in the dark streets.

He'd lost belief that any one thing, person, country could be better than another.

Szálasi had killed hundreds of thousands of Jews, and all they did was hang him in their own terrible Hungarian way.

Afterwards, balancing his glass of ginger beer in one hand, a plate of passionfruit sponge in the other, Rodney Bennett confronted Ida. World class! he said again. He wondered, did she hire herself out? He and Tikka and some friends from the golf club were thinking of putting on something special, like an old-fashioned *thé-dansant*. They needed a top-hole pianist.

Ida replied that her repertoire was entirely classical.

'I'd bet on everything I've got that you could play whatever you wanted,' Rodney said, bending low, looking into her eyes, dimpling. Weren't these New Australians always complaining about poverty? You'd think they'd leap at a chance to get ahead.

Especially members of her race.

'Yes,' Ida said, as if she read his thoughts. 'But I am very expensive.' She turned away. Elsa's father was waiting to speak to her.

'A prima donna, I'm afraid,' Rodney reported to Tikka. 'And, you know . . .' He lowered his eyelids and rubbed his thumb and fingers together. Tikka saw that she had lost the chance to ask Ida for the name of her dressmaker.

Jack Briggs's sister wanted to be introduced. It turned out that Nance had worked for fifteen years as a secretary at the ABC. 'The *Australian – Broadcasting – Commission*?' Nance said, slowly and clearly, to make sure that Ida knew what she meant.

'Of course,' said Ida. 'I listen, on the wireless.'

Nance's boss – Ida didn't catch his name – was in charge of the Concert Music Division. Did she have permission to give him Ida's address? Jack was beaming, stamping his feet a little, proud to bits.

'Yes,' said Ida. 'Thank you.' She nodded and turned away.

Why was it that the more praise and admiration she received, the smaller and sadder she felt? The courtyard was hardly a satisfactory auditorium. And her technique – she had a sudden image of Julia Marai, in the high attic room overlooking the Danube, shaking her head. How could she ever again attain the level she had once reached, here, now, living as she did?

The fact was, she had short-changed these people and they didn't realise it. She took a breath.

Strange that this should be the moment that at last she fully understood. This was the land in which her life would take place. In which her music must grow. This was her audience. The émigrés, the petit bourgeois, the nouveau riche. Some country folk. She must do her very best. She looked around for Meyer and Frank.

Meyer with a tray was serving all the children cool drinks, half a glass each, as requested by the nurses, since they were about to go to bed.

Frank was nowhere to be seen. Nor was Elsa.

An announcement was made: forty pounds had been raised for the occupational therapy room. During the applause, Frank and Elsa started walking up the exit ramp. Both in callipers, holding hands for balance, without a word they made their way down the hall and out onto the verandah. They were tired of being with other people.

How good it was to sit down side by side, alone, with the lights from the Netting Factory falling across their faces, its thudding beat like the heart of their existence. Across the road, familiar shapes of trees and houses were outlined in a darkness that seemed almost transparent. Far away, the lights of the city were a distant radiance, a promise of life to come. They were used to being on their own now. They no longer belonged to their families. The people of the outside world tired them.

They sighed with thankfulness to be together.

Being with Elsa calmed Frank. It was a relief not to worry any longer about his mother. He saw now that he had always worried about Ida.

'The long kind summer evenings,' he wrote in his prescription pad. 'More hours to be with you.'

They sat quietly with one another. For Frank, the music was still with him. To hear those pieces again was like a

169

reunion, though he would never tell Ida that. For the first time since he fell sick, he had a feeling of strength.

'Did you like the concert?' he asked.

'Yes. Your face is like your mother's.'

'Which piece did you like best?' He wanted her to put it into words so he could see if they felt the same.

'Mm. The first one.'

'Why?'

'Reminded me of "Twinkle Twinkle", I suppose.'

She didn't have a piano at home. While they were here he would start to teach her.

Once she'd belonged to the whole world, Elsa thought. Now she belonged with Frank.

23.

Albert

After the piano had been wheeled back into the schoolroom and all the children and the nurses were asleep, Albert Sutton, lying in bed, thought he would make a bolt for it. Now that he'd seen Lizzie and all his brothers at the concert, he knew he couldn't wait any longer. The missing was worse than being sick. It filled his head, made him stupid, he couldn't learn, couldn't even speak. Deep down, all through himself, he knew that only when he went home would he get better. All he wanted was to open the front door and hear them say, *'Allo! 'Ere's our Albert!* He'd planned to run away many times: how he would take a bottle of water, maybe an apple and a warm jumper. But tonight as he lay in the dark, a quiet voice told him: *Go now.* If he took his wheelchair and followed the railway line, he knew he would find his way. At least he no longer wore splints. *Just go*, said the voice.

He slid off his bed, sat on the floor in his pajamas and put on his shoes and socks. Hauling on the mattress, he pulled himself up again, slowly put on his jacket, and stuffed his dressing gown into a hump under the sheets. In a stroke of inspiration, he arranged his brown knitted cardigan on the pillow to look like the back of his head. Then he lowered himself into his wheelchair.

'Where are we going?' Little Lewis, in the next bed, sat bolt upright, his eyes wide open.

'Hush your mouth,' said Albert. 'I'm takin' meself off home.'

Lewis lay down again at once. Albert realised he was asleep.

He rolled out of Boys, down the corridor, through the hall, opened the front door and pulled it to, but did not close it because it made a click. He eased himself down the ramp beside the front steps so he didn't go too fast and tip over. He'd been thinking about these moves for a long time. Hadley was on night duty but she must be asleep on the couch in Sister Penny's office. He was rather fond of Hadley – his brothers teased him that he was sweet on her – and he had a funny feeling he wanted to say goodbye.

Just go.

The air was still warm. He could hear the chirp of crickets. He left the lights of the Netting Factory behind and rolled past the dark houses towards the railway line. The wheels squeaked a little, they needed to be oiled. When he got home he knew exactly where his brother Reggie's oilcan was.

At the railway line he turned left. At this point, unlike the railway line, which was down in a gully, the road climbed. Again and again Albert started off, but each time, halfway up, he was unable to reach the top. He knew he mustn't cry.

172

Suddenly his arms couldn't do it any more. He was so tired that he rolled off the road into the long grasses of the verge beside it. He put on his brake, climbed out and lay down in the dry, rustling grass. As the moon rose high in the sky he fell asleep.

When he woke it was still black night, and there was no sign of any cars. He remembered that when he rode Lizzie's bike, if you zigzagged across a road it made it easier to climb a hill. He propped himself up behind the chair and pushed it back onto the road. Sitting in the seat, pulling and pulling on the wheels, he managed to tack up the hill from one side to another. But near the top, when he paused for breath, he forgot to put the brake on. The chair rolled straight back. He managed to make it swerve backwards into the verge, tipping him head over heels into the grass. The chair fell on top of him. This time he couldn't move. He heard the wheels softly spinning above him. His leg hurt and his head felt dizzy. He thought he heard a motorcycle, and wondered if Reggie was coming to look for him. The sound passed. In a minute, when he got his breath, he would push the chair off, sit up and start again.

24.

Ann Lee

After the concert, and Albert's accident, everything seemed to change. The days were cooler, the light more tender, dry leaves rattled down the road past the Netting Factory. Albert was still in hospital while his broken leg mended. Sister Penny had been obliged to explain the incident in full to the Golden Age board of governors. After that the front door was locked at six each night. Some of the governors expressed incredulity that it had been left open, even though the citizens of Perth took pride in the safety of their town, never locking their cars or houses, sleeping on porches in summer, or even on front lawns.

Night-duty nurses were reminded that they must shine their torch onto every sleeping child. Hadley had red eyes for two days after Sister Penny had spoken to her. The incident continued to cast its shadow.

Every day during rest-time, Sister Penny visited Albert in Princess Margaret Hospital. She didn't want him to lose hope. She told him that as soon as his leg healed he could go home. She had spoken to his parents. His sister and all those big brothers would help with his exercises. Albert nodded. He was very serious and quiet. Everyone at the Golden Age, children and staff, was a little quieter, a little more sensitive.

In the classroom, Mrs Simmons began a social studies programme called 'The Great Composers'. 'We all know now about the power of music!' she told the class, with a special smile to Frank. She saw him flinch. She brought in records and played them on the old gramophone. This week's composer was Mozart. Because of the concert all the children had heard of him. She told them the story of *The Magic Flute*. Frank was allowed to have a free reading period on his bed during these lessons. Otherwise, as Mrs Simmons rightly judged, he might explode.

One afternoon someone came walking up the hall, boot heels clacking on the boards with a purposeful sound. It could only be a man. It was rest-time, silence reigned in the wards. Sister Penny was visiting Albert. The nurses were upstairs.

The girls on their beds listened to the approaching footsteps. The man knew where he was going. Next thing his face appeared, tanned the colour of mahogany shoe polish. He was wearing a big square brown hat, turned up at the sides with a fur strip around the crown.

'Annie? Ann Lee?'

Ann Lee lifted her head.

In three strides the man crossed the room, put his arms around the tiny girl and lifted her high into the air.

Elsa and Susan Bennett propped themselves up on their elbows. Julia Snow and Lucy Boyer lay still, their eyes wide open on their pillows.

'Can you walk, darlin'?' His voice was hoarse but gentle.

Ann Lee nodded. She wasn't smiling but beneath her fringe there was a look on her face that the other girls had never seen before. What was it? A look of complete satisfaction.

'Show me.' He put her down on the floor and backed three feet away, sitting on his haunches. She stood swaying in her little, much-washed white cotton shift.

'Come on, chook,' he said. He held out his hand. She took a step towards him and he backed away. 'Come on, come on,' he said softly, like calling a little bird. Step after painstaking step she made her way to him. Then he picked her up, whirled her around the room, his big-knuckled hand dark against her tiny shoulder. He smiled, curling up his eyes in the pained way that a man did when he was trying not to cry.

'Where are your things, Annie? In this cupboard?' He pulled a pair of overalls up over her shift and buttoned them. Then in one hand he held her old carpet bag and swept the contents of the cupboard into the bag with the other. He stood up, holding it. With the other arm he scooped up Ann Lee and clasped her to his side like a little monkey.

'Mr . . . er . . . Lee!' Sister Penny had returned and was standing in the doorway.

'Hafta get going, Sister. I've lined us up a lift to Leonora.'

'Can I have a word?'

He followed her, still clasping Ann Lee.

In her office, she said, 'Ann is making such good progress. The physiotherapist is very pleased with her. We're confident that in a few more weeks she'll be stronger in her walking.'

'It's enough,' he said.

Sister Penny looked at Ann Lee's face. She had lost her remote look. Her eyes gleamed. She wasn't smiling but a light had come on.

'We got the call,' her father said.

'What call?'

'Hers. Her mother and me, we both felt it. We were eating breakfast at the kitchen table. We looked up at one another and we said at the same time: Annie can't take it any more.'

Sister Penny smiled. 'She's been *perfectly* happy.'

'Time to come home.'

'Now?'

He nodded. 'The truck'll only wait for half an hour.'

There was nothing in the world she could do to stop him.

'Then I'll need your signature,' she said.

'What for?'

'Signing her out without a doctor's permission. So you can't blame us if anything goes wrong. And there's a list of exercises I'd like you to have.'

Sister Penny felt suddenly weary. Who knew, in this mysterious business of healing? Perhaps he was right to take her home.

The children were allowed to leave their beds to say goodbye. They gathered round the front door, excited by the glamour of Ann Lee's father, half-expecting him to carry her off on a horse. Her rescue had a storybook feel that made them light-headed, believing for a moment in their own imminent deliverance.

Ann Lee, held high, unsmiling, her black eyes expression-less, looked steadily at them over her father's shoulder, then turned away forever.

Sister Penny found it hard to smile. Ann Lee was going to be lame. Would more treatment have helped her? She would walk, but with a heavy limp. She would be known as a cripple. Crippled Annie. Annie the gimp. Would she ever get married? What would she do with her life out there in the desert?

Briefly her mind raced. Ann Lee was quick with numbers. Perhaps she could do the books for the mine manager . . .

But Sister Penny was less optimistic than she used to be. She went back and sat in her office. When did this start? Since Albert's accident?

It was her day off tomorrow. When she handed over to the evening shift, she told Hadley that she was going to the country for the night and wouldn't be back till late after-noon. She drove off straight away.

At the Golden Age there was a general sense of loosen-ing, of being left to one's own devices.

25.

Blue Air

By the time she'd crossed the Guildford bridge over the sluggish river and bowled along an empty road between flat stretches of paddocks, the sun had set.

The dog's barking started as she turned off down the long gravel driveway and reached a crescendo as she pulled up outside the house.

He came out onto the verandah in bare feet, shouting at the dog. She stepped out of the Morris. The dog leapt, whimpering and quivering on its chain. They stood looking at one another in the blue air, the moment of no-light just before the dark descends.

'Hello, Penny.' That's what he called her, her name as he'd first heard it, on the ward.

'Hello, Tucker.' It was a sort of recognition between them, of equality, self-sufficiency, that they addressed each other by surname.

'Come in.' His glance was even, levelling, but something about the way he turned and led the way told her he was glad she'd come. Down the hall, into the big farm kitchen, his shoulders high, his thin legs thrown forward stiffly. In bare feet it was almost elegant, the dance of a long-legged bird.

'How's your back?' She'd nursed him at IDB in the '48 epidemic. A sapper in the army, he'd survived the war to come home and catch polio.

'Not bad. You're in time for tea.'

His grandfather had built this house. Nothing changed here. The fire in the stove, the big wooden table, the wide, swept jarrah boards on the floor.

'Dinner?' He had a half-eaten plate of stew waiting for him on the table. She'd interrupted him.

'No, thanks. You go ahead. Just a cup of tea for me.' He made a mutton stew on Sundays and it lasted him the week. It didn't appeal to her.

She watched him eat. Right from when he was a patient, she had felt this peace with him. Whenever she came to this near-empty house with its vistas of flat paddocks running to the horizon, she understood why. After the war, he'd returned here and would never leave again.

It was peaceful too in the big iron bedstead where his parents used to sleep, where he was born. His father and mother and all the Tucker uncles used to be communists. There were no curtains in the bedroom window, which was wide open. She lay looking at the swift stars skimming across the black sky until her eyes closed. Hoots and barking echoed across the paddocks. She could smell the dry grasses rustling in the night air. In the morning the birdcalls would wake her.

She liked his smell, sundried, like the sheets. His back made it difficult for him, but she knew what to do. In the management of pain, he had been her first and best teacher.

He slept deeply, like a child, his breathing clean as the air. She could say to him, as to nobody else, 'I'm tired, Tuck.' It was as if she were lacking something elemental, a mineral like iron or salt. There was a flatness within her like a deflated heart. Perhaps that was why the landscape here soothed her.

She felt it as a lack, as if she were missing someone badly. Who was it? Ann Lee? Lidya? Her own daughter . . . ? What had captured her spirit? Somehow she kept returning to the night of the concert. The calamity of Albert, of course. But before that, something else. She saw herself standing up, announcing the forty pounds. During the applause, she had looked at Meyer Gold's face across the courtyard, and had seen, really seen, the depth of his detachment. Their eyes briefly caught, then, expressionless, he looked away. She hadn't seen him since.

So that was it! That was all . . . an invisible thread had been broken. A hum in the wires had gone dead. And yet, somehow, almost unconsciously, there had been a consolation, even a sort of trust, just in knowing it was there. Nothing had gone quite right since.

She heard a pattering on the iron roof. Rain at last. She shut her eyes firmly to sleep.

In the morning, Tucker sniffed the air. 'It's going to bucket down.' The sky seemed to darken as he spoke. There was a distant growl of thunder. Suddenly Olive felt that she must call the Golden Age. There was a telephone box in Guildford.

'We could certainly do with a couple of inches,' Tuck was saying. He put two bowls of steaming porridge on the table, and a tin of Golden Syrup. He rarely smiled but his long face fell into lines of deep benevolence. His river-brown narrow eyes were always humorous.

'I have to go, Tuck. I haven't time to eat.'

'What's up?'

'I don't know. The kids. I've just got a feeling . . . I must get to a phone.'

She looked around. She'd brought nothing with her, would take nothing back. Tuck followed her out to the car. He lived without expectation. Long ago he'd learnt to respect her intuitions. Besides, though he would snort if she told him this, he was a gentleman.

The little Morris sputtered as she drove back across the Guildford bridge – if she pushed it too hard it would overheat. But after the phone call, speed became the essence of the matter. She knew how things worked at the Golden Age like the functions of her own body. Every minute counted. If only Hadley wasn't in charge! After Albert, she was so intent on following correct procedures that the girl had lost all touch with her own reactions, her own common sense.

'I thought I'd better contact the governors,' Hadley had said on the phone.

'You didn't! Oh, for heaven's sake!'

Frank Gold had been found in Elsa Briggs's bed.

'Doing what?' Frank and Elsa. She should have known this could happen. She *did* know, but had been distracted! Should have left instructions to keep an eye out . . . They were in love. You couldn't afford to leave one chink open, or fate, accident, mishap, like infection, would step in . . .

Hadley swallowed. Her voice dropped. 'He was on top of her. They were sort of . . . undressed.'

The sprinkles on the windscreen grew heavier. Olive had to turn the wipers on.

26.

The Third Country

When did everything start to change? Suddenly Frank's face had become familiar to her. Not handsome, nor unhandsome, but like her own, a sort of twin, a mirror. Their connection seemed to fill the air around them. From the moment they woke up to the light glowing behind the long white curtains in their separate dormitories, they were waiting to rejoin each other.

What was it? Frank said it was like poetry. It felt right or it didn't. If it was given to you, you had to take it.

He said that it was love. The word 'love' did not scare or embarrass him. Every day he had new thoughts about it. It was like a promise made to all human beings, he said. It was the big thing, maybe the best thing, that happened in lives. He and she had received it very young. It was as if they had been blessed.

All day and night, Elsa thought about the things he said. Nobody else in her life – parents, teachers, Reverend Hollis in confirmation classes – had ever talked like Frank. It didn't matter what you said, he had an idea about it.

Being close made them stronger. They sat talking on the verandah or the back lawn. Their faces had colour. For some weeks now they'd shared the lonely task of rehabilitation, doing their exercises together. The Scottish physiotherapist commented on their rapid progress and motivation. The days were not boring, but seemed to hold at every glance something for them, something to tell the other. During the night they missed each other. Each morning was a reunion. If one of them had to go to Princess Margaret for a test or an adjustment, the other went silent, lonely as a widow or widower.

Two people living together were always learning about each other, Frank thought. Elsa knew about the ceiling and the piano lesson and the trains, though at first she didn't understand why the little boy Frank had had to hide. She didn't know that a disaster of biblical proportions had occurred while she was a tiny girl growing up in Swanbourne. Nor that ordinary people, neighbours, could kill each other. All she knew about the war was that Jack Briggs had been stationed for most of it on Rottnest, the little holiday island just off the Perth coast. He used to make a joke of it, called it his 'overseas posting'. The story of his life, he said.

Elsa's stories, by contrast, were all of freedom, of the sea and the neighbourhood. To buy fresh eggs meant dodging Mrs Hoffman's butting ram as you crossed her yard to the Kearns's place behind her. Alec Kearns was a war pensioner who raised chooks, grew vegetables and fruit trees. All the backyards were like small farms, except for the Briggs's, which was a wilderness.

The days were not long enough for all they had to tell each other.

Frank knew that he saw Elsa more clearly, watched over her more carefully, than anyone else. He loved the long days of existing with her. The sensation of belonging to her. What was happening to him was so huge, he hadn't yet found a way to write about it. He didn't have words for her, her shine, her dignity. He tried. A white swan. A golden plum. 'The Lover', the staff called him.

The title of the new poem came to him in a rush one night when he went back to Boys. Warren Barrett was dealing cards for a game of rummy with Malcolm Poole and Lewis.

'Wanna play?' Lewis piped up, always looking for Frank's support.

'Nah,' said Warren Barrett. 'He only plays with his girlfriend.'

Frank lay back on his bed and they forgot him. It was as if he lived somewhere else now. The title came back to him so clearly he could see it written in his head. 'The Third Country': now he saw that it was not one poem, but a set of poems. About the long journey he had made to find her. About the two devils, war and polio, that had brought it about, and the two angels, love and poetry, that had saved him. How Sullivan had showed him the way.

Every country had its rules. He had to learn them. How long would he be allowed to stay here? Was this the country where he could finally feel at home?

His mind raced with the happy play of metaphors. He lay oblivious, as Hadley came to tell the boys to finish their game, as the lights were turned out and the others fell asleep straight away. After some time, he sat up against his pillows in the beam of light coming from the hallway through the crack of the open door. He wrote in the prescription pad:

You are the first inhabitant
I meet
In this new country.

The words were coming now as they might not tomorrow. He filled a page. When he'd finished he felt tired, exultant. How quiet and dark it was. He could always sense when Sister Penny wasn't around. A hum went still. The engine was turned off. 'A ship without a captain': he could write another poem! He could write all night, he wasn't ready for sleep yet. He wanted to tell Elsa about it.

Afterwards he would think, was it such a breaking of the rules? There wasn't a sign on the Girls door to say: 'No Boys Allowed After Lights Out'. No one had ever told them that.

No boy had ever *thought* of it before Frank Gold, Sister Penny told the governors.

In the end it was decided that they must both leave. Elsa, questioned, didn't say that Frank had acted against her will. She didn't say anything at all. She had seen, when she came in, a collection of faces so old and grim, so marked by righteousness, puckered with disapproval, that their jaws drooped, their eyes hung down.

'Were you surprised when he lay on top of you? Were you shocked?'

Elsa shook her head with lowered eyes, as if she'd lost the power of speech.

She did not say: *I wanted him to*. How could she tell them that?

'Elsa, did he undo your pajama top?'

She shook her head.

'Who did?'

She shook her head.

'Frank says the buttons came undone "by themselves". How could that be?'

She sat looking down. *It happens when you lie against each other, face to face. It's friction, stupid . . .*

'You don't know?' They were gentle with her. She could tell it was Frank they wanted to blame. Why did everyone always want to blame Frank?

'Did you ask him to get into your bed?'

She shook her head.

'Were you shocked when he lay on top of you?'

Again she shook her head.

'Why not?'

'I don't know,' she whispered. They were intruders. She mustn't let them get anywhere near her and Frank.

'Did he touch you where you didn't want him to?' A lowered voice.

She froze. Shivers ran through her. How could they ask her that? It was *rude*. Worse, so very much worse, than anything she and Frank did. A word that everybody used to say at school came to her: it was *revolting*.

Their questions made her feel sick. Their minds made her sick. Why didn't Sister Penny speak? She was pale and quiet, as if a light had gone out.

'Thank you, Elsa,' the chairman said, smiling gently, as all old men always smiled at Elsa. 'You may go.'

191

Elsa took her crutches and left. She knew as she made her way back to her bed that she would never get over this. She found it hard to walk. Every muscle she had nurtured, tried to love back to work, shrank in humiliation. She felt as if clods of dirt had been thrown at her. Not by Frank, but by those old people on the board. She would never forgive them.

'I must ask you, Sister Penny, if you'd become aware of the physical nature of this friendship?'

'Not at all. There has never been any report of this behaviour.' Olive paused. 'You have to understand,' she said, 'that when children are cut off from their families and live side by side, they become very close. All the children are fond of each other. Elsa and Frank are the same age. They have both been here for more than three months. They are very good friends.' They become used to each other's bodies, she could have said. They work on their bodies side by side.

Really, she thought, children hoped for, longed for love in each other as much as we do. They needed to express it. Most kids hoped, however vaguely, 'to marry' one day.

'Hmm. Judging by their way of showing it, they are too old for this hospital.'

'Children can surprise you by how much they feel and understand. How mature – emotionally – they really are.'

There was a pause. Oh Lord! She was making it worse.

The governors sat unmoving, as if in expectation of her.

'I will speak with their doctors,' Sister Penny said. She nodded imperceptibly to herself, as if at last she'd hit on the course she must take. 'They have both made good progress. Perhaps they'll be able to go home.'

'In the light of what has happened,' said the chairman of the governors, 'I think that is the only possible course.'

He paused.

'First the little English boy. Now this. Are you sure the children are being adequately supervised?'

'I must reiterate,' said Sister Penny, 'that I have every confidence in my staff.' Apart from Hadley Dent, whom she could cheerfully sack . . .

But she knew, they all knew, that she should be looking around for another position.

27.
Poetry

Frank caught the tram to the big red brick state library. For weeks he went there and read every poetry book on the shelves. His need was so great that it forced him to leave the house. He plotted his route like a general before a battle. How he would mount the tram, how he would sling his bag over his shoulder and hold his stick, what he would do with his stick when he sat. Each morning he surveyed the sky for signs of the weather. If it looked like rain he stayed home. It would be too hard to navigate his way – he feared umbrellas, puddles, slippery surfaces. He had an image of himself flailing on his back like an upturned beetle.

He hoped he wouldn't see anyone he knew.

A librarian took an interest in him when he asked for poetry and brought books to him, even a few precious first editions out of storage. She was freckly, large-boned, dry-skinned, with short, thin, fly-away hair, so shy she managed to be almost unnoticeable. At first Frank wasn't sure if she was an old young woman or a young old woman. She was probably in her mid-thirties. A reader. Something she said once, about a friend who used to write poetry, alerted him.

'Has he published anything?'

'He died in Crete in forty-one.'

She was a sort of war widow, he sensed. Shirley, he heard her called. Finding books for him, directing him, made her dry, pink face flush. He wondered if his lurching gait, his stick, made him look like a wounded soldier. He liked that idea. He liked the square way she held the books, and the way she set them down in front of him. But some days, if he was tired, he didn't go to the library. He couldn't face Shirley's intensity and the stacks of books to read and understand. Like a young, exploring animal, he needed to graze slowly, alone, unnoticed, free.

Once he would have made friends with Shirley, found out everything about her. But since coming home from the Golden Age, a quietness had taken him over. He'd closed off, like someone after shock. Lost trust in affection, in being open to other people.

The silence at home made him aware of how much he was now alone. Passing cars and buses, the occasional clatter of heels along the footpath were not the solid heartbeat of the Netting Factory, the bustle in the corridors of the Golden Age. Late at night he could hear a lone wind suddenly rushing through the pine trees in the park opposite.

He woke each morning to the smell of coffee, as he always had. Passing through the shadows in the rooms, he felt he was going back to who he had been, his parents' child again, and the quietness in which they lived together.

But he'd been away a year. He was taller, he had pubic hair. He'd outgrown his clothes, outgrown the need for his parents' attention. They hadn't yet learnt what he now knew, that he, and only he, could cope with his condition.

He moved like an old man. Everyday living took longer than it used to, dressing, walking, making his bed. His mind had to plot out how to do it all. It made him tired. Something felt ripped out of him: his youth, his strength, his heart.

He hated his ugly shoes.

Everything had changed: his image in the mirror, his thin leg, his lopsided shoulder. His status, his future. He had no one to talk to, nowhere to go. He understood now how much being with Elsa had shielded him from pain. As if her beauty had sheltered both of them.

Before he started going to the library, he felt he was lurking in a half-life, unearthly, silent, adrift. Waiting for the tram in mid-morning, he saw he was on the other side now, with the old people, the damaged, those who were out of work.

Poetry was his way into the world. Poetry had to save him.

He sat on the front porch looking at Meyer's garden and tried to make up little poems about birds with broken wings, maimed insects eaten alive by ants. The poems stalled, as poems did when not left to speak for themselves.

It wasn't polio that had done this to him. It wasn't disgrace: his parents were only bemused by his expulsion. They shook their heads at the unintelligible morals of colonial Anglo-Saxons. A boy had gone to visit his sweetheart one night? But of course! Still, they had not stood up for him, argued his case. They were newcomers to this country, they must accept how things were done here.

It was the lack of faith in him at the Golden Age that hurt. The lack of love. Every single person there, child or adult, was vivid to him. He could never forget any one of them. He'd thought that he was close, in different ways, with each member of the staff. But they had all turned their backs on him. No respect was shown for the depth of his and Elsa's feelings, no trust in the truth of their love. Even Sister Penny, who saw and knew so much, had not stood up for him and Elsa.

He'd sensed a reluctance on the part of the governors and staff to expel Elsa. They wanted to believe it wasn't her fault, that he had pushed himself on her. But she'd refused to blame him, or deny her feelings for him.

She had gone to the stake for him. The only one to stand by him.

Carefully, he did not allow himself to think of the feeling of their bodies against each other, of her soft mouth against his, the fierce flutter of her heart. He would wait for her.

Day and night he carried this ache for her. Only with books did he lose his feeling of panic, of having been discarded, forgotten, thrown out.

In a few weeks, at the beginning of third term, he would start at Modern School. He tried to see himself objectively in Ida's wardrobe mirror. Small, pale, with pathetic spindly legs and the shoes of an old man: compared to all the high-school boys he saw walking past, a ghost, a creature from another planet. As for his face, he could hardly bear its nakedness, the searching eyes, the sadness, the consciousness of self.

He hoped that by the time he went there, he would have given up the stick, and if possible the shoes. Then, though he would limp, and sport would be out of the question, and though he could never run for the train or eat his lunch cross-legged in the shade of a tree, at least at a desk he might *pass*.

He, who had so quickly acquired an accent like the other kids, so carefully adapted his clothes to look like theirs, was now always going to stand out. Easy to think that this was his destiny, that he was marked from the start . . .

The library had three of the war poets Sullivan had talked about. Brooke, Sassoon, Owen. There was no American poetry, except for one copy of *Leaves of Grass*, which electrified him, the voice so modern, so simple and direct.

Not I, nor anyone else can travel that road for you.
You must travel it by yourself.
It is not far. It is within reach.
Perhaps you have been on it since you were born, and did not know.
Perhaps it is everywhere – on water and land.

He copied out the poem by hand.

Shirley told him of a bookshop, O'Harrell's, in Trinity Arcade between Hay Street and St Georges Terrace. For Frank this was a long journey over unexplored terrain, with new surfaces to negotiate and steps, escalators, crowds. He planned his route with the help of Meyer's road directory and set off mid-morning on a weekday when the streets were not yet busy. The city, in its depths, was surprisingly lovely, every open space filled with winter sunlight. O'Harrell's was up a staircase (never easy), a small narrow room with long dark polished shelves filled with modern books, English and American, a few Australian, some European translations. It smelt of tobacco smoke: the owner, Hal, was a chain-smoker.

Frank sensed that Hal understood the romance of O'Harrell's. He wore an eyeshade like a croupier and his shirtsleeves were shortened with stretchy metal bands. He showed Frank a thick novel by Dos Passos called *USA Trilogy*, which Frank instantly craved. Hal was small, middle-aged, with black greasy hair slicked back onto his collar, a lined face, stained teeth. He limped – a motorcycle accident, he told Frank. He could have been a bookie or a gambler. Instead he was the purveyor of miracles, as keen on tracking down these books as a hunter of rare prey. Did he read them? It was as if he didn't need to, he'd already absorbed their qualities, knew their value. He was their champion.

Frank knew, as soon as he opened it, that he must have *The Bridge* by Hart Crane. As he hovered over it near the counter, Hal said that he accepted lay-bys. Frank told Hal he intended to get a job. But for the time being he didn't even have a shilling for the deposit.

If he had not caught polio he would have had a job, he knew. Selling newspapers after school, running errands, sweeping out a shop. By now he would have been able to help his parents.

Hal cocked his head at Frank. 'D'you write the stuff yourself?'

'What? Poetry?'

'What else!'

'I do, yes.' Frank, flustered, longing to be taken seriously, searched his mind for lines. Only Sullivan's came.

I have to find myself
A place where I can breathe.
That's where poetry lives
In the oldest part of us.

Hal slowly nodded.

Suddenly Frank was overwhelmed by what he'd done. Plagiarised Sullivan! The friend who had introduced him to poetry! The one who would never find him out . . . A hot wave ran up his face. The lousiest of crimes. Not only that, bad luck! Sullivan had trusted him. The gods of poetry would turn their backs . . .

'Actually,' he said, 'that was written by a friend.'

Hal did not blink. 'He is interesting.'

'He had polio. He died.'

'I tell you what,' Hal said. 'If *The Bridge* hasn't been bought by the end of the week, I'll put it aside for you. You pay it off as you can.'

Tired after his poetry expeditions, Frank lay on the bed in his dark room. His eyes fell on the battered little prescription pad, now consigned to a place on the shelf along the wall beside his bed. Ever since he'd been away from Elsa, not a single genuine line, not a true poetic thought had stirred. He tried to write a letter to her but the words seemed shallow, false.

Meyer had built that shelf for him, so that everything was within reach, books, pens, a glass of water. It was waiting for him when he came home.

Frank found himself thinking of another father, the grieving Mr Backhouse. How much would he treasure the last thoughts of his son? As scribe and guardian of them, was it his, Frank's, responsibility to hand over those few first lines of Sullivan's to the rightful heir?

Before they found their way into his own . . .

He would like to speak about this with someone. But with whom? He still had not spoken of his poetic vocation with Meyer and Ida. Why not? Because they would want to read his poems. And they were only fragments really, he was like a poet who wrote in air.

It was not the sort of stuff they sometimes recited to one another in Hungarian. They wouldn't know why he was so sure. They might pity him, try to encourage him to take up something else – chess, crosswords.

He dreaded their loss of faith in him. These days his parents trusted very little to promise. They did not become excited about the future. Ida had spent years studying, practising her vocation. Now she was a milliner. They'd look sceptical about a few lines in a prescription pad. They'd smile with their mouths only, Ida would bite her tongue, they'd carefully put the battered little book down on the table and busy themselves with something else.

Already Ida had suggested that, if he studied hard, the law might be the best career for him, since it was sedentary.

He was their future.

The only person with whom he could have spoken about this, discussed the moral issues in detail, was the one he could not see.

Funny, in his thoughts Elsa was not a girl exactly. More like a spirit, a sort of radiant warrior . . .

He remembered the way she did things, talked and moved, ate and drank. Her kindness to the other kids, whom he could not be bothered with.

He closed his eyes into the silence. Did she too miss the heartbeat of the Netting Factory, the distant rush and whistles of the trains?

In memory the Golden Age had been an orchard of peace and light.

Some days when he woke, his emotions – fear, resentment, boredom, grief – were so present that if he was alone he didn't trust himself to get out of bed. He didn't know how he could make it through the long hours without breaking something, making something dark and violent happen.

He had to start to please the gods. He had to change his fate.

In the library, he asked at the desk with the Information sign how he could contact Government House.

One day he walked to the phone box on Fitzgerald Street and rang the number he'd been given. He was told that Mr Backhouse and his family had gone to live abroad.

'For good?' Frank's voice went high with surprise, revealing his youth.

'Yes.'

'There was something I wanted to give him.'

'I'm afraid we cannot give out a forwarding address.'

Yet if he could have seen Elsa, if he hadn't felt like such an outcast, an Esau, if he could have shared this recovery of the world, he might have enjoyed it. There was a new richness here for him – silence, and space and unexpected dimensions to people. The challenge to find out ways to do things would be like a game if it was shared.

He lay awake far into the night. Many things would happen to him in his life, he thought. But they would happen to a cripple.

Every night in bed, when she was sure Frank was asleep, Ida gave an account to Meyer of their son's condition.

'I hear him in the bathroom. He talks to himself in the mirror.'

Meyer knew that she worried about the melancholic streak that ran in his family.

'It's a rehearsal,' he said softly, staring into the dark.

'What for?'

'His new life.'

Ida lay silent for a few minutes. She sighed. 'Then there's the bar mitzvah class . . .'

'Give him time, Ida.' He turned his back.

One morning Ida left the wireless on when she rushed off to work. Frank, in bed, heard music starting up. Violin – if it had been piano he would have got up and turned it off. Notes were pelting out, patterns raining down, like voices calling to each other. 'Plaisir d'amour'. Its sadness made him shiver, the pain was almost luxurious. Frank pulled the blankets over his head and howled.

Meyer came out whistling from behind the lantana bush around the lavatory and slapping his newspaper briskly against his thigh made his way to the back steps.

Frank was sitting at the top of them. 'Home for you is having your own dunny,' he said. It was an old line.

Meyer, on cue, gave his response. 'Beats spending five years shitting on a freezing hillside next to twenty other men.'

That used to make little Frank laugh his head off. Not this time. Meyer saw that even in the morning Frank was sad. Not petulant or sulky, but resigned, as if he understood now what the world was like.

'The first sign of those who've given up,' Ida said.

Whenever Meyer thought of his wounded son, he rolled a cigarette. Inhaling, his breath hurt his chest.

28.

The Hunch

'How did you find me?'
  'I had a hutch.'
  'A hutch?'
  'A feeling, soo-per-nat-ur-el . . .'
  'A *hunch*!'

It was true, he'd made a delivery to the grocery in Swanbourne, then his hands and feet seemed to make the decision
for him: he was driving down North Street, heading towards
the ocean. Somewhere along here Feri's girlfriend lives, he
thought, though that was not the reason for the detour.
This whole area was suddenly charged with an almost erotic
interest for him. He felt he was heading into a story, something already written. He wanted to see how it would end.
At the top of North Street the ocean spread out before

him, and turning right into the dead-end gravel road above Swanbourne Beach, he was hardly surprised to see the little Morris parked there. Standing on the kerb, beside the open passenger's door, Olive Penny, her full, round, pale thighs and arms revealed in an apple-green swimsuit, was looking down, slapping sand off one foot and then the other with a towel.

Still in the dream, not quite sure that he himself hadn't conjured up this vision, he pulled up behind the Morris, and climbed down.

'Now I know why the ocean was *ir-res-istible* today,' he called, walking towards her along the kerb, his hands turned up as if a message had come down from the heavens, almost hating his European charm. The winter sun suddenly emerged from behind a bank of cloud, a white brilliance that engulfed them, so blinding it was almost comical. Using their hands as visors they loomed, dreamlike, squinting at each other. Hard to know if their mouths were stretched into a smile or a grimace.

Like this, her hair slicked back, her broad, ruddy face pale from the water, her limbs firm and smooth, she looked like a big, strong sports-playing girl. But he did not miss the slight puckering above her knees, her wide, knobbly feet, a vein snaking down the inside of her left calf. Her skin was lightly freckled across her chest. She reached into the car and pulled out sunglasses and an old white towelling beachcoat and briskly put them on. Her hair grew lighter by the minute, tossing in the wind across her face. She took a pin out of her beachcoat pocket and skewered the front of it into a roll back from her forehead. A practical movement, yet in some way glamorous.

He had an image suddenly of sitting with her at a table in one of the little cafés overlooking Lake Balaton. On the table wine, rolls, pickles; around it brothers, their girlfriends, guests from Budapest. The peace of couples who have been swimming and then taken a siesta together in the afternoon. Everyone easy, cheerful, sensual . . . Such a capacity she had for living. A purity about her, as engrossed in life as an insect going about its tasks . . . embedded in all that is natural.

The sun was submerged again behind a cloud and they could speak.

'I wanted to talk with you,' he said.

'Yes?' Her head tilted in query, the professional.

Could she hold it against him, that his son had helped bring about her dismissal?

'Where do you go next?'

'To Darwin. I've accepted a position as Head Sister in the Infectious Diseases Ward.'

'With children?'

'Children and adults.'

'Don't go sailing in the ocean there!'

A black joke, in bad taste . . . His heart was racing. Why? For loss.

She did not smile. 'No, indeed.'

He hunted around. 'And your daughter?'

'Engaged! Married next month.'

'Off your hands . . .'

'More like I'm off hers! Elizabeth Ann has been swallowed up into what she's always wanted – a big, respectable family.'

'You do not look so pleased.'

'*I* have a hunch . . . That she's pregnant.'

Meyer knew enough about society here to understand that this was very frank. She trusts me, he thought. Or else I don't matter enough to count . . .

'That puts a girl at a disadvantage. Especially with her mother-in-law. Anyway, how's your son?'

'He is too quiet. Lost some confidence, I think.'

'Illness is humbling,' Olive said.

'He's . . .' Meyer put his hand out, palm up, and pressed the air. '*Heavy*. Sad.' He fumbled for a cigarette, his head turning as he lit it.

'He misses Elsa,' Olive said flatly. 'They were very close.'

How easily he took the sun, she thought, looking at the leather-brown hollow in his smooth cheek. The sea breeze blew about in the soft, thinning nest of black hair at the back of his crown. His brow furrowed for a second as he drew in, all the lines showing in his dark face.

'It's not all bad, you know,' she said. 'There's an awareness in these children, way ahead of their years.'

Meyer said nothing.

'Frank needs her. They were good for each other. They shouldn't be kept apart.'

Where to go from here? Meyer thought. The wind blew, the light blinded, the road ended. The sea roared below. Soon she would leave and very likely they would never meet again. They would forget each other, as so many had been forgotten.

He wanted to give her something, tell her something. She deserved better, as the truly good always do.

'You know,' he said, 'I learnt from you.' Above the wind, his raised voice was hoarse.

'What did you learn?' She was suddenly still, unreadable behind her sunglasses.

'How to live here.' If he stepped towards her now, they would not part. They stared at each other so steadily that in the whiteness they became each other's ghost.

Olive started up first, made a brisk u-turn, drove past him, waved. Plenty of time to think about him, she thought as she drove off. Years and years.

All the same, something that had oppressed her ever since the governors' meeting – an intuition perhaps that loss would always run like a seam through her life – seemed to have lifted, been carried away in the sea wind.

He was a little magical. Once or twice she'd met people like him. An old Scottish woman she'd nursed to the end once told her that in a past life she, Olive, had been a pilgrim trudging along a road, a lone knight.

He knows where to find me, she thought.

She looked in her rear-vision mirror and saw that the truck had also pulled out, was making a three-point turn, much faster and more recklessly than a big truck really should.

29.

The Call

Ida came home early from work one day to find Frank sitting on the back steps, his chin in his hand, his elbow propped on his knee. Beside him was the poetry book he'd been carrying round for the past week now, *The Waste Land*.

'What are you doing out here?'

'Listening to a bird,' Frank said, without looking at her.

'Why?'

'If you listen long enough to a bird call, it tells you something. Listen!' He held up a finger. 'There it goes again. One long note then four short ones.'

'What does it tell you?'

'*You're . . . just-in-the-way*,' Frank said, staring ahead. '*You're . . . just-in-the-way*.'

213

Ida stood still. It felt like the time when the tanks rolled in, and you thought, *This can't be happening.* Everything becomes provisional. She walked straight out of the house to the phone box on the corner and rang Margaret Briggs.

30.

The Separation

In the afternoons while Jane slept, Margaret massaged Elsa's legs with warm oil on the kitchen table, stretching and bending them as she'd been instructed. She could hear the Scottish physiotherapist's voice purring in her ear: *Lait yu-err hunds take oh-vairr.* She looked out of the window over Elsa's head at the new vine leaves tossing bright green over the trellis, while her red hands did their work on these poor limbs.

Washing went unhung, dishes lay piled up on the sink and Lord knew what she'd put on the table for dinner, but for Margaret, doing anything for Elsa was a holy task, a blessing.

'Oh Mrs B.,' the women said in the butcher's. 'Your poor girl is home at last.'

'And doing very well,' Margaret said with dignity, remembering how they had turned their backs on her at the counter, how they had whispered about Elsa. She would never forgive them, not for herself, but for their shunning of Elsa.

There wasn't much she trusted these days. Not hospitals. Not even God any more. Only the love between parents and children.

It had given her the strength to put Nance in her place. Nance had kept on turning up every few days at the house.

'At least she won't have that migrant boy hanging round her now,' she said. No one had told her about Frank but Nance had a nose for that sort of thing. Elsa disappeared into her room. Nance announced that she was going to pay for Elsa to go to PLC for two years, and then to secretarial college.

'She couldn't go to a co-ed school, not now,' Nance said.

'But Elsa wants to go to the university,' said Margaret. 'She's going to be a doctor.'

'Oh, for heaven's sake!' said Nance. 'Look at her! Whatever would the patients think? And it's more than likely she'll never marry. She needs to be able to support herself with a quiet, sedentary job.'

Margaret rolled and unrolled the tea towel she was carrying.

'As a secretary she could probably get work with a charitable organisation,' Nance went on. 'If I were you—'

'You're not me, Nance,' Margaret said. She'd wanted to throw the tea towel at her sister-in-law, but as usual had just missed her chance. The red veins throbbed in her cheeks and her blue eyes blurred with furious tears. 'And you're not my family.'

'I beg your pardon! My brother—'

'A family is a mother and a father and their children. Thank you very much for your help but we don't need it any more. The bank's giving Jack a loan for a second-hand Hillman so he can drop Elsa off at school.'

Late that night, in her bed on the back verandah, Elsa heard her mother outside in the dark hanging out the nappies, singing softly to herself.

At first Elsa was dazed, taken over by the chaos and profusion. It was nearly a year since she'd left home. In hospital there was a strict routine, and all the surfaces were clear. How simple it was to live there, how light she'd felt!

Here every window was filled with heaving greenery, like being underwater. Home was a burrow of small, dark rooms, filled with people's moods and feelings. You moved between light and shadow. At any time someone could cry out. Meals were noisy with likes and dislikes, her mother trying to please each one of them. Elsa wondered why she'd ever thought she missed her family. She became exhausted and retreated to her room. Her room was her salvation.

Before she'd come home, Jack had enclosed the louvred part of the back verandah with a plasterboard partition. Margaret hung a bedspread in the doorway as a curtain. There was her bed and a little table and a chair for Elsa to do her homework. The louvres rattled in the wind and the verandah creaked as if it were tugging at its mooring. Some nights when it was quiet, Elsa thought she could hear the surf's roar way down at the end of North Street, like the echo of a shell held to your ear. She woke to bird chatter, rooster calls, the baaing of Mrs Hoffman's sheep. In the afternoons when the sea breeze came in, the yard was alive with rushing light and frantic leaves.

There were her old books, and old photos of herself, straight-limbed, carefree. Even her smile had changed.

At some time each day the winter sun through the louvres seemed to gather into a single point across her bed. She lay in wait for it to reach her, imagining it as a searing, healing ray of light.

The winter rain thundered on the corrugated iron roof. Her life was lone and perilous, a tiny ship in a great ocean.

Jane's cot was moved from the parents' bedroom into Elsa's old space in the bedroom with Sally. As if for consolation, or in revenge, Sally was rarely home, racing off on Malvern all around the district, on errands for Margaret or adventures with her friends. If home Sally slammed a tennis ball against the garage door – THUNK, THUNK – for what seemed like hours. In that way she also escaped feelings of pity for Elsa, for her pain, her limp, her silence.

Elsa used crutches now only when she went outside, where surfaces were unreliable. Once a week she went for physiotherapy at Princess Margaret Hospital, catching the train, walking with crutches up Thomas Street. She never saw Frank in the grounds of Modern School, nor in the physiotherapy waiting room. She looked for him though she knew he wouldn't be there. Each time she came home exhausted.

She limped unaided around the house, like a bird with its wing broken. Tame, because it couldn't fly away. All her time was taken up with managing herself, working out new ways to do things. Being a different person in the world. As often as she could she went out to the backyard. The outside calmed her.

She observed her mother going about her tasks. Although Margaret sighed and her legs ached, her days were a rich mix, a grazing from one pleasure to another. The crop of mint by the back drain. The magpie she fed. Dusting the family photographs in the lounge room, each one lovingly picked up, wiped like a child's face. Behind her was a trail of half-done tasks, and Fat Jane wrecking what was left.

Still Margaret sang to herself. She told Elsa how, as a war bride, she used to push her in the pram right up North Street to the sea, to point out to Rottnest, where Jack was stationed. When she came to live in this house, she said, for the first time in her life she was happy.

Her parents never said a word about her expulsion from the Golden Age. Nothing could affect their shining gaze on Elsa. But they hadn't tried to stick up for her, they hadn't saved her. She saw them differently. They had no power. They cared what other people thought.

At night, she lay stiffly. Every part of her had shrunk and been offended. Judgement had been passed on her, like a blow across her neck. She was disgraced. But underneath she knew she had a right to what she felt.

Frank was the only person she had ever known who spoke about feelings. More and more now she felt as if part of her were missing. She and Frank had been ripped apart. At night in her room she felt him with her. Did that mean he was thinking of her? Was he, too, sick with missing her? Out in the world he was more confident than she was. But deep down, she sensed, more woundable.

In her head she went over and over what had happened, as if she were discussing it with him. She gave reports to him on every member of her family. She thought of writing him a letter but how would she post it? She didn't even know his address. He didn't have a telephone. She fell asleep clutching her pillow.

One day when her mother had taken Jane with her to the shop, Elsa went into her parents' dark bedroom and opened the wardrobe. On the back of the door was a long mirror. She put the light on and saw a thin, flat-chested girl with a clunky brace on her left calf, one shoulder higher than the other, the once fluid lines of her body now distorted. She was surprised by her eyes, their intensity.

She used to hear people say, 'What a pretty girl.' Now they'd say 'the crippled girl' or 'what a shame'.

The need to talk to Frank made her want to lie down, pass out. She didn't know if she could get through this alone. From the moment she woke till she fell asleep at night she did nothing much else but think of Frank. She lived only for him.

Day after day the sea breeze swept up North Street, the washing danced on the line, the sun set through the louvres. Jane patted her big sister's face with her starfish hands because she knew she was sad.

In the ship of her bed, Elsa dreamt and dreamt, as if the thin verandah walls were permeated by the moon and stars. One night she dreamt she woke, left her bed and walked smoothly, unaided, a normal girl again, across the verandah to the top step and stood looking out. The moon filled the yard with a dark silver light. Around the corner from the driveway came a line of children following each other like leaves blowing along a gutter. A small boy was running beside them, desperate, worried, urging them along. For some reason, she knew that he was Sally. Sally with her new sense of responsibility for them all, as she, Elsa, had once felt.

Elsa was sitting on the verandah steps shelling peas for Margaret one sunset when Sally came rattling up the driveway on Malvern. A string bag full of groceries swung off the handlebars. She carried it past Elsa on the steps.

'Sally!' Elsa said, looking up at her.

'What?' Sally said.

Their eyes met and held for a moment. They hadn't looked at or spoken directly to each other for a year. They stared so hard that they could feel the start of tears at the back of their eyes.

Still Elsa could not speak. But it was enough.

'Hmph,' said Sally and went inside.

Elsa would never know how much her mother grieved for her. Her shoulders, as Margaret massaged them on the kitchen table, were thin and bowed like a young widow's. Too much had happened to her too early. No young creature should have to feel this sorrow.

The telephone rang. Margaret rushed to answer it before Jane woke, wiping the oil from her hands on a tea towel.

'Oh! Mrs Gold,' Elsa heard Margaret say. A shock ran through the length of her body, stretched out from one end of the table to the other.

'Yes,' her mother was saying. 'Yes, all right then. Three o'clock here, tomorrow.'

As Margaret put down the phone, there was Elsa standing in the hall in her singlet and knickers, her long frail legs shining with oil. These days Elsa heard everything. Being home for so long, she knew exactly what was going on in the family. She picked up signals like a wireless.

'The Golds are coming for afternoon tea,' Margaret said. How had this happened? To her, who dreaded visitors? What would Jack say? Would he want Frank coming here? And the house a mess . . .

'Mrs Gold said she would bring a cake . . .'

Elsa walked unaided to her mother and for the first time since she'd come home, kissed her.

31.

The Visit

Out of the white glare of the afternoon, three figures came walking from the direction of the station and were now crossing North Street. A man and a woman holding on to their hats as the sea breeze swept in, and between them the slight figure of a boy with a stick, limping.

Sally raced inside shouting, 'They're coming!' and slammed the front door behind her so they could ring the bell and arrive properly. Visitors were rare in their house. Nothing this exotic had ever happened here before. Elsa's boyfriend and his family! Europeans!

Frank and Elsa stood facing each other in the hall for a moment, while his parents were ushered into the lounge room.

'You're taller.'

'I can't write poems any more.'

He always talked first about himself.

He wanted to tell her everything at once. Oh, the relief to see her! Their eyes blurred, their lips seemed to swell. They couldn't speak.

But he was also registering everything around him. After all those hours of talking, laying out their lives in vast, historical detail, everything seemed half-familiar, as if he'd been here before, or dreamt it. The hallway smelt like Elsa's blue woollen cardigan at the Golden Age. His eyes fell on a carved wooden trunk and he remembered that Auntie Nance had given it to her brother Jack after her trip to India.

'The camphor wood box! To keep the moths out of your clothes . . .'

Elsa broke into laughter. 'You never forget anything!' Her eyes were bright, like an excited little girl's, her teeth white as milk. Frank wanted to kiss her.

'Come on, they're waiting,' Elsa said.

Frank sat next to Meyer, hooking his stick over the arm of the couch. Elsa sat across the room, on the bench beneath the windowsill. Elsa too had grown. She was still half an inch taller than Frank. A tall, very slim girl, with a limp and a brace, and the face of an angel. Meyer looked sharply at her, the evenness and delicacy of her features, their planes luminous against the pale light of the net curtains. Had she sat herself there on purpose?

No, he thought, she doesn't want attention. He noted the simplicity of her movements, her self-possession. She's learnt all she needs to know about her condition, he thought. Her family hasn't kept pace with her, all the things she's learnt.

She feels at home here, Frank thought. His stomach clenched suddenly at their distance.

Ida too was drawn to her, the beautiful thing in the room. It was dark and cluttered here, like the parlours in row houses in the north of England. Once, as a schoolgirl, she'd sat in rooms like this with her father, when he had taken her with him from Hungary to England on a pre-war business trip – Leeds, Manchester and Liverpool.

She made herself smile a little, to fend off the sinking feeling that these rooms had always given her. Next would be the rattle of the tea-trolley . . .

'Are you going to school now, Elsa?' she asked, her red mouth stretched, encouraging. Out of the wish to put on a good face for Frank's sake, to show respect for this family, she had curled her hair, pencilled her eyebrows, worn her hat with the net, unintentionally making herself even more formidable.

'At the start of third term.'

'What school?'

'Princess May, in Fremantle.'

'A good reputation?'

'Yes.'

Elsa had a way of floating away from questions, Meyer thought. Her blonde hair and pale face seemed to melt into the light. An angelic grasp of appearance and disappearance . . . He could feel Frank next to him, very still, on guard for her.

Frank was surprised by a pang of homesickness for the Golden Age. The freedom of orphans . . . How natural it had seemed. He remembered the feeling of power.

Margaret poured tea from her best teapot on the little table in front of her. Black for the Golds, who each stirred in a couple of teaspoons of sugar. Margaret's hands shook and her blouse kept coming undone over her large breasts. Jack blinked, cleared his throat, blew his nose. Sometimes he couldn't help seeing his wife as a sort of animal – dumb, fearful, intractable, or else lost in strange transports of joy. At the mercy of her feelings. Her femaleness embarrassed him. While Elsa, swift and reserved, was the son he'd never had . . .

Roszi! Once again Meyer's heart lurched. Of course! Margaret had always reminded him of his little sister. The only girl in his family. Like their mother, she served the men. As much as her brothers were dark and dashing, Roszi was short, round, buxom. Pink cheeks and a chignon at the nape of her neck. An innocent. She sang as she went about her tasks. After their mother died, she took on the running of the house. She refused to leave Balaton, managed to hide out with her father in the forests. One day when her surviving brothers were making their way home from work camps or out from hiding, she had gone to the lake to bathe and the Russians came. Their father was shot. Someone had lied to them that he'd served the Germans. Roszi was raped to death.

Was Margaret loyal like his little sister, loyal unto death?

The younger, red-haired Briggs girl, cheeks flaming, handed round a plate of lopsided floury scones. Obviously Elsa was not yet agile enough for this task. She still wore a calliper on her left leg.

At least with this family there was no need to fend off pity.

Strange Australian rituals, Ida thought. These thick floury breads that stick to the roof of your mouth. Breakfast food.

And the peculiar custom of being invited into a bedroom to lay your hat and coat across the sagging marriage bed!

The baby, Jane, was sitting on a rug next to Ida, drooling over a rusk. The child was fat and short-haired, her eyes like slits above ballooning red cheeks.

'The picture of health,' Ida said, baring her teeth. A contrast to Jane's slender nervous sisters, her serious father, her tired mother . . . This huge baby had sapped them all.

Jane caught Ida's eye. Confident of love and admiration, she clapped her chubby hands for her and jigged, her chins wobbling. Ida stretched her lips for a moment, clapped once or twice, looked away. Suddenly Jane began to howl and her mother took her off to bed.

She knew I didn't take to her, Ida thought. The whole family was sensitive and highly strung. Frank should take care.

How shy all the Briggs were! Flushed, serious, clearing their throats, in every word attempting to be honest. Meyer's eyes shone. He loved families, loved identifying family traits. But how did two such different ones come to produce children who had fallen in love with one another? Ensured the mixing of the blood, he supposed.

Always, it seemed to him, Australians resisted the social arts, apart from the pub, or these terrible tea parties, when what was needed was a glass of brandy each, and everyone sitting around a table. Preferably outside, under a big tree, with light and little leaves streaming down all around them . . . He longed for space, for air, right now! To escape these uncomfortable rituals. The floral china teacup, the matching saucer and plate, the polished fork and starched napkin all balanced on his knee. Oh, to be sitting on his own front porch, with a glass of brandy, playing cards by himself.

Margaret bravely cut into the cake that Ida had brought. Everybody took a piece. Something changed then, a brightening that was visible, as the consolations of chocolate and brandy, coffee cream and vanilla, of meringue and fine egg sponge appeased the spirit of each one of them. The Briggs family had never tasted anything like it. An Austrian torte, from Klein, the Jewish baker in North Perth, the Golds said. As good as anything in Vienna.

A generous contribution, Jack thought. Meyer Gold, driving a cool-drink truck, would clear, what? Twelve pound a week?

All the same, Ida thought, wiping her mouth, warmed by the success of her gift, there is something modest and quiet about this room. Everything blends in, has meaning: the big brown wireless, the shelf of old books, the watercolours of the paperbark trees beside the Swan River. The framed photographs of the shy little girls with their plaits and coaxed smiles, their big new teeth. Their heartbreaking innocence.

The light had changed. A grey stillness, like suspense, filled the room. Jack Briggs looked towards the window. Leaves began to rustle. The lace curtain gently stirred. He cleared his throat. 'Rain's on the way.'

'The washing!' Margaret jumped up and without apology ran from the room. Only the immensity of her task, keeping Fat Jane in dry nappies, could override her duties as hostess.

They all stood up at once, as if called to a task, and without a moment's hesitation put down their plates and cups and hurried after her along the hall, through the kitchen, across the verandah, down the steps, past the grapevine to the washing line, where Margaret was snatching at nappies. The sky arched up around them, huge, glowing, black, as if they'd entered a great cave. Thunder rumbled discreetly like a giant's indigestion. All the greenery was aglow. Everyone ran to help. Like revellers in a crazy dance, gasping, laughing, they grabbed at the worn, stained squares, the pegs rattling into a tin pail.

Nature has won, Meyer thought. As it always does here.

He stood looking around him. How well they lived! A bank clerk with a family and a backyard as big as a market garden. From here, with all the neighbours' trees around the boundaries, it looked like a meadow lying fallow. If there was one thing this country had to offer, it was land.

The vision seemed to come to him out of the sky, unfolding like a cloud or a flock of tiny birds, the outline spreading and contracting. A smallholding, a tiny farm. With ploughing, fertilising, watering, he could pasture a goat on a block like this, grow fruit trees and vegetables, feed his family from the land.

It was what his father had done. What he was meant to do.

Once you work the soil, you belong to it.

For so long now he had passed over the surface of the earth like wind over a desert, like shifting sand.

Elsa knew she had to get Frank away. While the others milled around the washing line, she headed out through the flimsy yellow grasses, giant thistles and wild oats, to a hidden place at the back fence where the dense, green foliage of the neighbour's peppermint tree hung so low over the pickets that it made a tiny room on the Briggs's side. Here you could sit in private on wooden fruit crates which she and Sally had put down there years ago. Nobody could see you. They used to call it 'the den'.

Just as the light broke out again, Frank came ploughing after her. For a moment the grasses shone silver, like ashes. Funny, he thought, taking care with the placement of his stick, the air has gone still. As if the world was holding its breath for them. Now he was with Elsa, a calm had descended over him. Everything was happening as it should, he thought.

'Let them go,' thought Meyer, glad that no one followed them. For once he didn't feel a pang of sorrow for their infirmity. Passion, for one who could no longer be host to it, was a gift, wherever it was bestowed. This time, they were the lucky ones.

'You can't just switch a feeling off,' Jack Briggs thought, turning from the line to watch them. 'Doesn't matter what anybody says.' He remembered Nance's carry-on when he told her he was engaged to be married. He picked up Margaret's washing basket and when he looked again the two kids had disappeared into that damned branch that hung over the back fence. Suddenly he felt tired of the whole business. He wished they'd all go home.

'Quickly!' Elsa's face appeared through the peppermint tree fronds. She couldn't help grinning. At last she felt restored to what she'd always known herself to be – a leader, daring, ruthless, even a little comical. She drew him into the den. Rain began to fall in light gusts.

The thick strings of leaves swung around, enclosing them in flickering darkness. With a long sigh they put their arms around each other. They fell at once into the fit of each other's body. Frank's stick toppled and was caught in the swaying green fronds. Raindrops spattered on the roof of leaves just above their heads.

Even in Elsa's arms, her face against his, Frank's body started to shake and sweat. He knew he couldn't stay here. It flashed through his mind that whatever this force was, it would never release him, it would take all of him. He would always be alone. The rest was make-believe, like this childish play-house, with its cracked cups and fruitbox seats . . . He closed his eyes.

But out of this moment he feels Elsa's arms suddenly release him, she is holding his hand, leading him firmly outside. He takes a breath, opens his eyes. They set off back together through the grasses to the others, small lurching figures beneath the luminous sky.

New York

An old man with a cane opens the door.

Even when he was very young, Jack had been aware of Frank as a presence in his mother's life. He used to peer at the pale boy with the sharp features and air of fierce alertness in her tiny brown Kodak snaps of kids on a verandah in the 1950s. But it takes a moment to recognise Frank in this melancholy, translucent face. The exuberant curls that once sprang back from his forehead have faded to a straggling grey. His nose seems more prominent, his full-lipped mouth is heavy and down-turned. He's wearing a loose black cotton jacket, like a dust coat, a grey shirt and grey tie. Elegant, in a bohemian way.

'Come in, come in.' He stands back, ushering Jack inside, his eyes never leaving Jack's face.

A large bay window is the source of light for the room. It's like a tiny enclosed verandah that juts out one floor up over the sidewalk, with a view in both directions of the street. Bright leaves tap at the upper panes from the black-trunked tree outside. Late afternoon, the room is leaf-shadowed. A built-in bench seat follows the shape of the window and is covered with papers and books.

'My desk, my office, my hearth,' Frank says, as he goes to clear a space on this seat for Jack. 'My contact with the world.'

There's an armchair facing the window, and an open bottle of red wine with two glasses waiting on a small table beside it. Frank hooks his stick over the back of the chair, sits down, pours the wine, and raises his glass to Jack, who, understanding only too well the careful planning of all this, raises his.

Everything in this room speaks of work and solitude. A desk with laptop and printer, a black mesh ergonomic chair. Bookshelves lining two walls. In one corner, a small bench with a kettle and cups and a microwave. Notes and photographs on a pin-up board. He remembers a line from Frank's last book. 'All those I live with are unseen.'

Jack.

'Your grandfather's name,' Frank says. 'Jack Briggs.'

The young man looks surprised.

'There was a time when your mother and I told each other every detail of our lives.'

Was his name Elsa's choice? His hair is pale blond, her colour.

Like this, seated across from Frank, the late afternoon sun falls onto features that are heartbreakingly familiar, high forehead and gentle chin, pale skin faintly pitted, as if by sensitivity. For a moment, Frank can't speak.

A creature of the light: his mother's son.

It's a pleasure to observe his repose in listening, his attentiveness, eyes alive with curiosity and humour. Qualities that will warm Frank for hours afterwards.

To himself, Frank calls him the Emissary. He has come a long way, from a place Frank left nearly fifty years ago.

'How is Elsa?'

Since she retired from medicine, his mother is much alone, Jack says. He's the youngest by ten years of three sons, and has always been close to her. Born when she was nearly forty. They are the readers in the family. She's the person with whom he discusses books. His brothers are both doctors, like their parents. Jack is a literature student. The family home is one street back from the beach, not far from North Street where she grew up. She used to walk up and down the sandhills and swim every day of the year, but is no longer able to. She refuses to be carried. His father has had a watchtower built for her at the top of their house, with a little elevator to reach it. The view is of the sea stretching out to the horizon, and far along the coast to the north and south. Apart from seeing a few old patients, she spends most of her time now in her tower.

'As I do in mine.' Frank gestures at his window, at the tree and shadowed brownstone opposite.

*

After a moment he asks, 'Does she ever speak of me?'

'When you send her your books. I borrow them from her. She's spoken of that hospital where you stayed as kids.'

'The Golden Age. She never writes back.'

Yet in some way, all his poems have been messages to her.

His mother is tough, Jack says. His brothers call her E.B., her initials before she was married. Once she makes up her mind, the family knows, E.B. never changes it.

Suddenly Jack finds himself telling Frank about a memory of her which is, he realises, never far from his mind.

He was going for a run along the beach when he saw her. She was climbing the sandhills after a swim and almost didn't make it. Went up three paces and slipped back two, over and over again. He knew he mustn't go to help her or even let her know that he'd seen her. The rule was that nothing was ever too much for her. By the time she reached the top, he was half-angry, half-crying. She lay sprawled there, unmoving, for several minutes.

Frank listens, nodding.

For years he too walked without a stick, raced along sidewalks, up and down flights of steps. Taught all day at Cooper Union, partied all night. Rejected any offer of assistance.

Their progress was always parallel.

You never know who your readers are, he thinks. His last book had only recently been published when he received an interview request from an Australian online journal. He has to admit that he was warmed by this acknowledgement, from a country that he left fifty years ago.

Or, rather, it turns out, acknowledgement from this young man, Jack, who seems to be the founding editor, distributor and a major contributor to the magazine. Well, good for him! But he can't help smiling when Jack speaks. The magazine is called *Praise*, but to Frank's ear now, in Jack's flat antipodean vowels, everything he says sounds right on the edge of irony. His voice returns Frank to back lanes in North Perth, bare feet, black sand between the toes. He feels the little churn in his stomach that means there's a poem for him there.

'What happened between you and my mother?'

'After school, Elsa went to Adelaide to study medicine. I qualified as a teacher and was sent to Eastern Goldfields Senior High School. Outer Siberia! At least I saved some money. Elsa met your father in Adelaide and got married. She wrote to tell me and soon after I left for New York.'

They sit quietly, as a small switch of leaves dips and brushes against the glass.

It seems to Jack that the room is alive with shadows.

'A few years after I came to New York, my parents died. First my father, my mother a few weeks later. Both buried the next day, according to our religion. Buried in the earth which my father had come to love. I never did make it back there.'

'They were both younger than I am now,' he says after a while.

Jack, in editor mode, his phone switched on to record, asks Frank to explain the significance of the title of the book he has just published. Why is a book of poems about children in a hospital recovering from polio called *The Golden Age*? While acknowledging that this was in fact the hospital's name, was his use of it as a title ironic?

Why does the poet say that he learnt everything he knows there?

Frank ignores the questions and announces that he has just published, with a small press, a book on Sullivan Backhouse called *Polio and the Poet*. It includes all Sullivan's poems and an autobiographical essay by Frank about meeting Sullivan, and the learning of a vocation. He gets up to fetch a copy for Jack.

'Sullivan opened a door to a world where everything had meaning,' Jack reads, the first sentence of the essay.

The book has a cover of a man standing with his naked back turned, waist-deep in glossy black water.

'I'm still trying to finish the poem called: "On My Last Day on Earth".' Frank smiles. 'Still waiting on the final line.'

He knows he's trying to avoid an interview. He wants to say, *Tell me about yourself. Have you been in love? Do you enjoy sex?* These days he likes most the light art of chit-chat about earthy things, like villagers in the square.

What is important to him? He knows the answer, it's everybody's answer.

He sits down again opposite Jack.

Suddenly it came back to him, he tells Jack, the beauty that was there. Elsa, the nurses, those fresh-faced girls. Sister Penny, that marvellous woman. The smell of hot bitumen roads on summer nights.

'The Golden Age' is the sequel to his most famous poem 'The Trains', he says. It's the answer to it, the counter to it.

He tells Jack how he came to write it.

He fell in love with many people, but always lived alone. Except once. With Edie. Edie was a revelation. She was eight years old, the daughter of a friend who had caught TB and had to go to hospital for several months. There was no one to look after Edie. So Frank said that he would take her. He would manage somehow, he said, swallowing dismay for the freedom and solitude he would lose. But he couldn't bear to think of a little girl with nowhere to go, or sent to live with strangers. He had no experience of child care.

He loved it at once! He discovered he had a talent for it. He was brisk, bossy, earthy, cheerful, and simply bypassed all unreasonable behaviour. He listened to her, and encouraged her to tell him stories. His eyes twinkled at her jokes, he could be genuinely entertained by her. She told him whoppers about other kids and showed him dance steps she'd made up, and liked to rub his cheek with her hand when he tucked her in.

He loved her croaky voice, her solid little body, her toasty smell when she climbed into his bed in the morning. They enjoyed Saturday mornings eating pastries and reading the *New York Times*, and going to the Met, or for a walk in Central Park. Her trust in him, her honesty, her joy to see him when he picked her up from school broke his heart.

How easy it is to love a child, even one who is not your own, he thought. And suddenly he was overtaken by memories of the Golden Age again after all these years – of the corridor and the verandah and the steady beat of the

Netting Factory and flocks of wheelchairs, and the affection of the nurses and Sister Penny, of Nella and Norm, Lidja and the Scottish physiotherapist.

Polio is like love, Frank says, a little abashed because he has pronounced this before, often, and in at least two poems. Years later, when you think you have recovered, it comes back.

Jack's plane leaves at midnight. He has to set off now, hail a cab.

'Did you find out what you wanted to know?'

'I did, yes.'

Frank doesn't take his eyes away from Jack's. They have a look of his mother's tonight – a dark centre, private, sad. Life hasn't begun for Jack yet. He's shy, a watcher, a listener. But there's nothing this young man isn't able to understand.

Jack thanks Frank one last time. He pats his bag, in which are copies, each inscribed, of Frank's six books. In spite of plans and promises, he's not sure that he and Frank will meet again. Like his mother, the poet is frail.

Not until Jack has reached the bottom of the stairs can Frank bring himself to close the door. He goes straight to his window, just in time to see Jack's bright head enter the stream of the crowd and swiftly disappear.

Acknowledgements

Grateful thanks to Jan Lord for allowing me to read a pre-publication version of her chapter 'The Golden Age – Aftercare for Children' in *Poliomyelitis in Western Australia: a History* by Tessa Jupp, Jan Lord and Lesley Steele; also for her encouragement and conversation. Thanks to those who composed the pamphlets for the Post Polio Reunion 2005, which were produced by the Post Polio Network of WA Inc.: 'Looking Back on the "Golden Age", 1952–1954' by Joy Hornidge; 'Memories of the 1950 School Monitor' by Briony Waterhouse; 'Memories of IDB Iron Lungs and other things', by Norma Clarke, Isabel Lutz, Margaret Shoesmith and Marjorie Olsen. And to Ann Martyn for her story about the thirsty horses.

Thanks also to Noel Avery, Daniel Brown, Kate Brown, Nikki Christer, for her continuing support, Catherine Hill, for her perceptive and scrupulous editing, Harry Hohnen, Isabel Huggan, Eveline Kotai, Tom Kurtak, Georgette Langley, Drusilla Modjeska, Sheryl and Sam Salcman and the helpful assistance at the Makor Library, Andor Schwartz for his memoir 'Living Memory', Baba Schwartz, Kathy Temin.